## Shock hit ██████
## like a tidal ██████

Roland was st██████████
arms, his long fingers ██████████

"I'll be leaving tomorrow," she said shakily, "and if you lay one finger on me I'll—"

He laughed at her. "Oh, I'm really frightened," he mocked. "You made a dangerous mistake coming here tonight, English girl." His eyes were sheathed in ice, yet on fire, too.

"You're crazy!" Christabel burst out. "Or drunk!" she added, and he laughed again.

"You think I'd have to be drunk to want to make love to you?"

She flinched, her amber eyes filled with hurt. How could he be so brutal to someone he hardly knew? Then she thought with even more shock and pain...what had happened to the man to make him like this?

**CHARLOTTE LAMB** began to write "because it was one job I could do without having to leave the children." Now writing is her profession. She has had more than forty Harlequin novels published since 1978. "I love to write," she explains, "and it comes very easily to me." She and her family live in a beautiful old home on the Isle of Man, between England and Ireland. Charlotte spends eight hours a day working at her typewriter—and enjoys every minute of it.

## Books by Charlotte Lamb

HARLEQUIN PRESENTS
1001—HIDE AND SEEK
1025—CIRCLE OF FATE
1042—KISS OF FIRE
1059—WHIRLWIND
1081—ECHO OF PASSION
1106—OUT OF CONTROL
1170—NO MORE LONELY NIGHTS
1202—DESPERATION
1236—SEDUCTIVE STRANGER
1290—RUNAWAY WIFE

HARLEQUIN ROMANCE
2696—KINGFISHER MORNING
2804—THE HERON QUEST
2950—YOU CAN LOVE A STRANGER

Don't miss any of our special offers. Write to us at the following address for information on our newest releases.

Harlequin Reader Service
P.O. Box 1397, Buffalo, NY 14240
Canadian address: P.O. Box 603,
Fort Erie, Ont. L2A 5X3

# CHARLOTTE LAMB

## rites of possession

*Harlequin Books*

TORONTO • NEW YORK • LONDON
AMSTERDAM • PARIS • SYDNEY • HAMBURG
STOCKHOLM • ATHENS • TOKYO • MILAN

Harlequin Presents first edition March 1991
ISBN 0-373-11345-5

Original hardcover edition published in 1990
by Mills & Boon Limited

RITES OF POSSESSION

# CHAPTER ONE

CHRISTABEL leaned her face on the train window, her amber eyes vainly searching a darkened landscape for clues as to where they were. They had left Paris in sunlight, she and the two little girls, excitedly staring out at the changing countryside for a long time, but shortly after they crossed into Brittany Dani and Nina had fallen asleep on the seat opposite her, curled up like puppies together. Christabel had read her book for a while until Dani yawned, half opened her eyes, and mumbled in sleepy French, 'Are we there, yet?'

'Not yet, not long now, though,' soothed Christabel in the same language, and the child let her heavy lids droop again. Christabel looked at her watch. Nearly ten o'clock! She felt it should be later. They seemed to have been on this train forever. She turned to stare out of the window then, and saw nothing except an occasional gleam of light from a cottage or farmhouse. They must be nearing the coast, but although she had lowered the window she could not yet smell the sea.

It was a remote and lonely countryside they had come to, and she thought again, as she had thought several times during the journey...what if there was nobody at the station to meet them?

Don't even think it! she told herself, and picked up her handbag. She got out a powder compact and gazed at her reflection in the tiny mirror. She hated what she saw in mirrors: the thin, intense face; the pale olive skin, and the mouth which was too wide and too big; the yellowy amber eyes which she thought odd and had never seen on anyone else; the dead-straight brown hair she wore bobbed short.

Well, she wasn't going to win any beauty prizes, and Roland de Bellème was not going to take the slightest notice of her, anyway, so why should she bother how she looked? Defiantly, she combed her hair, put on a dusky-rose lipstick, brushed a trace of blusher on to her pale cheeks.

The train was slowing down. She took another look out of the window. As they followed a curve in the track she saw ahead the lights of a station, and at last caught a fleeting scent of salty air.

Jumping up, she began to collect their luggage together. The little girls woke up, rubbing their eyes and yawning. It was way past their bedtime and they were exhausted by the hours of travel.

'Are we there?' This time it was Nina, the younger child, who asked in a sleepy voice, and Christabel nodded at her, smiling.

'Do you want to go to the toilet before we arrive?'

They both said yes. They were nervous, which wasn't surprising. It had been sprung on them so suddenly, this visit to an uncle they couldn't remember, who lived in a place they had never seen.

'Well, be quick!' urged Christabel, and, staggering a little, they rushed to the lavatory. By the time they returned the train was drawing into the station, and Christabel anxiously stared out along the platform without seeing anyone waiting. When the train stopped the few other passengers alighted; Christabel got out first, helped the children down, and then lifted out the two suitcases and the overnight bag.

She looked around, but there was no sign of a porter on the platform and all the other passengers had vanished through the booking-office hall.

'Where's Uncle Roland?' Dani asked, shivering. This was July, but a distinctly chilly wind was blowing through the pines bordering the station, and Christabel bent to zip up Dani's anorak and lift the hood over her fair hair.

'We'll go and find him,' she reassured, mentally crossing her fingers. Their mother had wryly told her how difficult Roland de Bellème could be— what if he hadn't bothered to meet their train? She gave the children a false, bright smile, picking up the two cases. 'Not long now, darlings!'

Dani, who was eleven years old and felt that that was very grown-up, picked up the overnight bag, which was not heavy, and walked ahead. Little Nina, barely nine, half leaned on Christabel as they followed Dani.

'Why couldn't we go with *Maman*?' she asked for the hundredth time, her lower lip trembling, and Christabel again told her that it had been impossible.

'*Maman* has gone to Martinique to make a film, you know that!' Eve-Marie de Bellème was a loving if absent-minded mother; she had forgotten to renew the children's passports when they had lapsed, which would not have mattered but for a chance opportunity she felt she could not turn down. The film part wasn't a big one, but it was the first offer she had ever had; she felt she had to take it even though there was not time to get new passports for Dani and Nina.

She had tried to persuade Christabel to stay on in the Paris apartment for a month, but Christabel had been away from home for almost a year now. She hadn't gone home at Christmas because Eve-Marie had begged her to stay over that holiday; it was becoming a habit with her to be reluctant to let Christabel go home, and it was time to be firm. Before Christabel became the family au pair Eve-Marie had had a succession of unsatisfactory girls to look after the children while she worked in the theatre. It wasn't easy for a working mother to go out each evening not knowing for sure that her children would be safe while she was gone; Christabel sympathised, she liked Eve-Marie, who was a friendly, easygoing woman. Nevertheless, she had her own life to lead. Their arrangement had been intended to operate only during term times at the Sorbonne, where Christabel was studying French literature and art. Eve-Marie was supposed to get someone else to take over during the vacations so that Christabel could go home to her own family.

Well, the summer term at the Sorbonne had ended, her vacation had begun, and she was dying to see her parents, her brother, his wife and new baby, and her older sister. It seemed such ages since she had last seen them. Regretfully she had had to refuse Eve-Marie. She would have suggested taking the little girls back to England with her, sure that her parents would have welcomed them with open arms, and Dani and Nina would have loved the Wessex coast where her parents lived, but the passport problem made that impossible, too. Eve-Marie had tried to find someone suitable to look after the girls in Paris, and failed, making Christabel feel very guilty. She had been on the point of changing her mind and agreeing to stay, when Eve-Marie had told her that she had managed to persuade her brother-in-law in Brittany to take the girls.

'But he won't come to Paris to collect them. I told you how he hates leaving Brittany these days, didn't I?' Eve-Marie had said, and Christabel had nodded curiously, remembering all she had heard about Roland de Bellème.

'Will you do me just one little favour? I hate to ask it, I know how good you've been, and that you want to get home to England, but just another couple of days...if you could? Take the girls to Brittany for me?'

Christabel hadn't taken in what she was being asked at first; she was too busy thinking about the strange, difficult man whose brother had been the children's father. Eve-Marie had had a minor role in one of his plays last year and Christabel had been several times to see it, taking the little girls along to applaud their mother enthusiastically. Roland de Bellème's work had a cutting edge to it, a bitter twist to characters and events which she had not been too sure she enjoyed. The play certainly hadn't been boring; it had stayed in her mind, indeed, long after that night. It remained there now, haunting her, and she wondered just what sort of man the playwright was to create such disturbing characters.

'Will you, please, Bel?' Eve-Marie had persisted, and coming back to the small apartment and the noise of Paris traffic passing in the boulevard below, Christabel had realised what she was being asked to do.

Of course, she had agreed. It would clip two days off her own holiday, but she could easily get a ferry from Brest across to the west of England, and catch a train or coach from there, and it would be a little adventure. She had never seen Brittany; it would be exciting to catch a brief glimpse of it before she sailed for England.

It would be intriguing to catch a brief glimpse of Roland de Bellème, too. She had heard so much about him, yet none of the rumours and myths added up to a clear image; he was a dark, puzzling figure. It would be fascinating to be able to form her own picture at last. He had never been to Paris during the two years she had been living in his sister-in-law's apartment.

When Eve-Marie appeared in his play last year, the producer had tried desperately to get Roland de Bellème to Paris for rehearsals, or to appear on the first night, but both his and Eve-Marie's pleas had met a blank wall. Nothing would persuade the playwright away from his isolated *château* near the Brittany coast.

At least he had agreed to take his nieces for a month; he couldn't be completely cut off, Christabel thought, hurrying into the station hall, her feet thudding on the bare wooden floorboards. One uniformed porter was busy shutting up. He turned blank-faced to take their tickets.

'*Monsieur*, is there anyone waiting for passengers from Paris?' Christabel asked, in her fluent French. 'We are to be met here.'

Shaking his head and shrugging in that very Gallic gesture, the man said that he had not seen anyone waiting. 'Outside, perhaps?' He waved them towards the exit, obviously only interested in locking the station so that he could go home himself.

Dani ran outside and Christabel slowly followed, guessing what she would find—no sign of anyone waiting in the car park beside the station.

'*Monsieur*, is there a taxi service?' she asked the porter, turning back towards him.

He sighed, his expression morose. 'There isn't a taxi there? Well, then, he has gone down to the Place de la République. He meets the trains, and then if nobody needs him he drives down into the village and parks near the *auberge* to pick up anyone who has taken too much wine with dinner.'

Christabel grimly looked into the darkness beyond the station. She could see the lights of the little town, but there was a shuttered look about the streets—nobody about, few cars, everywhere closed and quiet.

'How far is that to walk?' she asked, irritated by the eagerness with which the porter answered.

'Down the hill, you can't miss it.' He couldn't wait to get rid of them.

The children looked aghast. Nina was almost tearful. 'I'm tired, Bel; I can't walk any further!'

'I thought Uncle Roland was meeting us,' said Dani, just as pale and weary. They had inherited their mother's corn-coloured hair and blue eyes along with her theatrical temperament, but at this moment both of them were drained of energy. Nina was a see-saw character, up one minute, down the next, but Dani was usually more down to earth, a helpful, friendly child. Christabel had grown very fond of them, and she felt a jab of anger with Roland de Bellème as she anxiously considered the two pale, drawn faces.

Why wasn't he here? How could he be so thoughtless as to leave them stranded at a railway station in a strange town at this hour of night?

The sound of a rather ancient car engine wheezing up the hill made the porter brighten. 'Ah, here's Pierre now. Tell him where you want to go and he'll take you.' He stepped out, slammed the door behind them all, firmly locked up and walked off, whistling.

They stood together, shivering in the wind, as the ramshackle old taxi jerked to a stop beside them and a tortoise-like head was thrust out of the driver's window. 'Are you waiting for me, *madame*? Where do you want to go? The hotel?'

Only one hotel? thought Christabel gloomily, but never mind—if they could not find Roland de Bellème they would surely be able to find refuge at the hotel for one night. This was the summer season, and there might be tourists taking a quiet seaside holiday, admittedly, but this was not a famous resort, nor a busy one, from the look of it. The railway station was old-fashioned and tiny, it seemed that there was only this one, very old taxi—there was obviously no night-life here to attract the younger holidaymaker. No doubt the people who did come had been coming here for years and liked the nostalgic feel of the place, the palpable sense of it not having changed since the turn of the century, which she had already picked

up. With luck they should be able to get a room
large enough for them all to share. She did not feel
easy about letting the little girls sleep in another
room. She would prefer them to be under her eyes
all the time. Her sense of responsibility was strong,
and she had promised their mother she would take
good care of them.

She smiled politely at the taxi-driver. 'No, we are
looking for a local house...you probably know
Monsieur de Bellème? Monsieur Roland de
Bellème, the playwright?'

The wrinkled old face was blank, the black eyes
like raisins sunk in brown, overcooked dough.
'Bellème, *madame*? No, I don't think...'

Christabel couldn't believe it. Roland de Bellème
was one of the most famous contemporary French
playwrights. Any taxi-driver in Paris would
probably have recognised the name and she was
certain that here, where he actually lived, he must
be even better known. He must surely be the most
famous local resident? Her face flushed angrily, her
voice rose. 'He lives at the *Manoir du Sorcier*! Just
outside the town, I was told, on the cliffs.'

The taxi-driver shrugged. 'I am sorry, *madame*;
I don't drive outside the town, you see. I only drive
people around in town.'

Nina began to cry and the old man leaned further
out to stare quite kindly at her.

'Tired, *chérie*? It is very late, *n'est-ce pas*?
*Madame*, why don't I take you and your little ones
to the hotel, eh? They're half-empty, plenty of
rooms, and very comfortable rooms, too. It isn't
smart, but they will look after you, give you nice,

soft beds for the night, and a good croissant and chocolate for your children in the morning.'

'They are not my children.' Christabel said, and he stared, crinkling his eyes up to see her better.

'Ah, *pardon*, *mademoiselle*. My eyes aren't so good these days, and in the dark ... well, I didn't see how young and beautiful you are.' His teeth showed in a doggy grin.

Christabel ignored the flattery, and told him, 'I am only looking after the children for their mother. I've brought them down from Paris to stay with Monsieur de Bellème, actually. They are his brother's children.'

The well-weathered face changed, the black eyes peering closer at Nina and Dani. 'Really? They are Monsieur Hilaire's children? He had two little girls, I remember. I saw them when they were babies. So it is you, is it, little ones? But where did they get hair that colour? That is not the Bellème colouring. There's an old rhyme they chant around here! "The Bellèmes, no angels ... must be devils. They're black of hair, black of eye and black of heart."'

The two little girls listened with sudden interest. 'It doesn't rhyme,' Nina pointed out, and the driver grinned at her, his few teeth yellow and broken.

'Nor it doesn't, *ma petite*, but that's how it goes!'

'I thought you said you had never heard of Monsieur de Bellème,' said Christabel drily, and the old man made a graceful gesture of apology, one gnarled, blue-veined hand lifted, while he grinned at her unashamedly.

'I am sorry, but sometimes reporters from Paris come down and pester Monsieur, you understand. He does not wish to be disturbed, and he is one of us. The Bellèmes have lived in the *manoir* for many years. Monsieur Roland grew up here. If he does not wish to see anyone, we aren't going to betray him.' He climbed down and picked up the two heavy cases with surprising ease, considering his advanced years, and lifted them onto his luggage-rack.

'It is not far to the *manoir*; a ten-minute drive out of town.' He held the door open for the two little girls, who scrambled into the back of the taxi, but did not forget their manners, politely thanking him.

'My pleasure, little ones,' he said, and aside to Christabel, 'Take after their mother, do they? She must be a beauty. Monsieur Hilaire married an actress, didn't he? A pretty blonde, judging by her daughters!'

Christabel picked up a distinct odour of sheep, hay and manure as she climbed into the front passenger seat of the taxi, next to the driver, wondering what passengers he had been transporting lately, two- or four-legged? But what did it matter? Beggars could not be choosers. They had no other way of getting to the *Manoir du Sorcier*.

'Will you be all right?' she asked the children, who yawned, nodding, past words.

'Poor little things!' said the taxi-driver, starting the engine, which spluttered reluctantly, coughed, wheezed, making the whole taxi shake like a dog after swimming. 'How far have you come today?'

'Paris.'

'Paris? Ah, no wonder they are so tired! I went to Paris once, on the train, oh, it must be thirty years ago. It took me a day to get there, and I came back by the next morning's train. Couldn't stand the place; all those people, bad-tempered lot, and who can blame them? I would be bad-tempered if I had to live in a town that size.' The taxi lurched off into the night, and Christabel gripped hold of the door-handle, hoping they were going to arrive in one piece. The car shuddered and groaned its way up the hill, away from the town, turning on to a winding cliff road with the sea on one side and open, heathery land on the other.

'Monsieur de Bellème was supposed to meet our train,' Christabel said, staring down at the Atlantic ocean far below the cliff. It glittered as if the moonlight shone on the points of a million drawn swords, and the wind blew her the angry roar of the waves rushing up on to the jagged shore. This was a violent landscape illuminated by the moon; the sheer, plummeting cliffs, savage rocks, great lofty crags towering above them. 'You haven't seen anything of him tonight, have you?'

The driver shook his head. 'But I'm not surprised he forgot to come; it's typical of him. He hates having visitors.'

'Oh, look!' cried Dani behind them, her voice awestruck, and Christabel followed her pointing finger to the Gothic black outline of a house which was just looming up above a great stone wall, beyond which lay a tangle of windblown thorn trees and pines which had hidden it until this moment. She had stupidly taken the stone wall for some natural feature of the landscape, a rocky spur thrust upwards from the cliff.

Swallowing, Christabel looked at the driver. 'That isn't . . . ?'

He nodded. 'The *manoir*,' he agreed cheerfully.

'Now I know why they call it the *Manoir du Sorcier* ...' murmured Christabel, with her eyes following the mysterious threat of the black, conical towers, the high, narrow windows which could admit little light, set as they were in the walls like arrow-slits, the forbidding gateway to reach which you had to cross a wooden footbridge over a moat. This was no ordinary house, intended for family use; it was a place built to withstand a siege, to keep the world shut out.

'Is our uncle a wizard?' asked Nina in a thready little voice.

'Don't be silly,' Dani said. 'The *château* has always been called that. A long, long time ago there was a lord of the manor who was supposed to be a wizard, but I expect he was just cleverer than everyone else. *Maman* says that in the old days people thought you must be a witch if you could read and write, because almost everyone was too stupid.'

'I don't think they were stupid, Dani,' Christabel said in gentle remonstrance. 'Nobody had educated them, that was all. Someone had to teach you to read and write, didn't they?'

'I can read and write,' Nina said, beaming with pride.

'So can everyone now, stupid!' Dani told her scornfully. 'I'm talking about really old times, years and years ago.'

'Were you born then, Bel?' Nina asked, wide-eyed with interest.

Christabel laughed. 'It was a little before my time, *chérie*!'

The taxi-driver chuckled wickedly. 'Even before mine!' He turned his yellow-toothed smile on Nina, who looked rather alarmed, burrowing backwards into the musty-smelling seat of the cab.

'Have the Bellème family lived here for long?' Christabel asked him, and he gave her one of his grimaces, nodding furiously.

'This branch of the family have been here since the sixteenth century. The Bellèmes were foreigners, of course!'

'Foreigners?' Christabel repeated in bewilderment. 'It's a French name, surely?'

'It's a Norman name,' the driver said, spitting sideways out of his cab. 'The Bellèmes came from Normandy... a wicked lot, they say, up to all sorts of dirty tricks in the Middle Ages. Some younger son—back in the reign of our King François the First—caught his wife in bed with one of his brothers and killed the pair of them, then fled overseas and stayed in exile for years. When he returned to France he didn't go back to Normandy, he came here. Oh, a wild, remote place Brittany was in those days, they say. Just the place for a man with a price on his head. The French king's law didn't run here—unless he sent an army down!'

'Was the murderer from Normandy the wizard who built the *manoir*?' asked Christabel, fascinated, but the driver shrugged.

'Maybe, I can't remember. It's an old *château*, but exactly who built it, I'm not sure!' He was driving up a narrow, winding road towards the towering gateway. The taxi's wheels grated over a sandy surface; the road was not made up, and Christabel grabbed the door-handle nervously as she bumped back and forth, narrowly missing being thrown through the windscreen. Nina gave a squawk of protest, but before Christabel could get out a syllable the taxi braked violently and the driver pushed back his peaked cap, rubbing his nose with one skinny, rather grubby index finger.

'Well, we're here. I'll carry your cases for you over the footbridge. Can't get my taxi over there, too narrow.'

They all tumbled out and stared up at the rearing black shape of the *manoir*; there was a light on in a downstairs room, Christabel noted with relief. The children's uncle was home. She was going to tell him a thing or two when she saw him. He had given her a bad hour since they had arrived at that railway station.

The driver marched on ahead, a case in each hand. He stopped at the closed gates of the gateway and put down the cases, then seized a long iron bellpull which hung down beside the gate. Far away they heard a strange, hollow clamour. The bell was ringing somewhere inside the *manoir*.

'Goodnight, ladies,' the driver said with cowardly haste, beating a retreat towards his taxi before Christabel could catch hold of him.

The taxi reversed, tyres grinding the sandy road, and drove off down the clifftop road towards the town. The driver waved a hand in their direction as the children stared after him. His voice drifted back to them, blown like a rag by the wind. *'Bonne chance!'*

'And *bonne chance* to you,' muttered Christabel, pale with weariness and nerves. How much longer was it going to take Roland de Bellème to come and open this gate? It was getting colder by the minute. The moon went behind a cloud and the wind roared past, catching their clothes, whipping them about, blowing their hair everywhere, throwing sand into their eyes, making them half-blind.

Nina began to cry. 'The wizard isn't going to let us in!' she sobbed, and Christabel bent to put an arm around her, hugging her.

'*Chérie*, don't cry, everything will be OK, you'll see!'

'Maybe he isn't home?' Dani suggested, her voice a little shaky too, although she was being as brave as she knew how, her small chin high and her backbone straight.

'If that taxi-driver hadn't rushed off, we could have driven back into town and stayed at the hotel tonight!' thought Christabel aloud, and at that moment they all heard a sound which made the two children shrink closer to her, their small hands grabbing hers and holding on tight.

'What's that?' quavered Nina.

Her eyes searching the shadows around the *château*, the crowding darkness of the pines and hawthorns, Christabel heard the sound again, recognised it, the grate of a shoe on gravel or sand, the sound of someone or something breathing. 'Someone is coming. Let's hope it's your uncle!' She hoped she sounded unworried, she did not want the children alarmed, but she was not as calm as she pretended. This was a wild, isolated part of the coast, and as far as she knew there was no other building within view or even earshot. If they screamed, who would hear them?

The noises were coming nearer, were louder, and now it was clear that there was more than one person coming towards them, out of the woodland.

Out of the dark bounded an enormous black hound with eyes that seemed to glow like coals. Nina, who was frightened of dogs, gave a choked scream and turned to run away, which was the worst thing she could have done.

'Stand still, darling!' Christabel hurriedly said, but Nina was past hearing her. The great dog bayed excitedly and began to race towards them, his tongue hanging out as he panted. Sobbing and stumbling, Nina ran on, and Christabel did the only thing left to do. She jumped into the path of the running hound and made a grab for his thick, studded leather collar.

'Don't touch him!'

Christabel's startled stare flashed past the dog to his master who came striding towards her, a black waterproof cape blowing around him as he came, his black hair whipped back by the wind, his black eyes furious. She remembered the taxi-driver's little rhyme... 'black of hair, black of eye and black of heart'. This member of the Bellème family certainly ran true to type, at least as far as the first two requirements were concerned. Was he black of heart, too? she wondered.

'Call him off, then!' she shouted back as she reached for the dog's collar.

It growled, deep in its throat, black lips curling back to reveal its fangs, snapping at Christabel's hand which she hurriedly withdrew just as its master shouted to it.

'Down!'

As if shot, the great hound dropped down, lay flat on the ground, head on paws, looking like the Sphinx and watching its master with intent attention.

'Good boy!' he congratulated, ruffling its rough black head, and the dog then relaxed, proudly sitting up and grinning.

'You shouldn't allow that damn great dog to run around without a lead,' Christabel shakily protested, keeping a safe distance from those sharklike jaws. She still did not feel very safe. 'One of the children could have been seriously hurt. It was going for Nina before I stopped it, and if it had bitten her——'

'I have Caesar well under control, as you saw!' its master said coolly, quite unrepentant. 'And Caesar was only doing his duty, protecting me and my property from strangers and intruders—which brings us to the crucial question...what exactly are you doing here at this time of night? If your car has broken down——'

'I'm Christabel Paget and I've brought your nieces from Paris——'

'My what?' the deep, dark voice grated and she stiffened.

'You . . . you *are* Roland de Bellème, aren't you?' There was a tremor of uncertainty in her voice now.

He stared down into her thin, pale face, his brows a jagged line above those antagonistic eyes, looked from her to Dani and then slowly turned to stare at Nina, who had crept back to Christabel's side to hold her hand so tightly that she was almost cutting the circulation off.

'These two?' he said harshly. 'My brother's children? My God, are you telling me she sent them after all? I told her I couldn't have them here. This is no place for children, especially little girls. There's nobody to look after them, and I don't have the time to do it myself. I wrote back to their mother telling her categorically that it was out of the question for them to come here, and if she ignored my letter that's too bad. I'm not changing my mind. It is impossible for them to stay. You will have to take them back to Paris.'

## CHAPTER TWO

'BACK to Paris?' Christabel couldn't believe her ears. 'I can't take them back.' She felt Dani move to the other side of her, slide her little fingers into Christabel's hand. This was very upsetting for the children; she must get them inside and out of this cold night air, out of earshot of this worrying discussion with their uncle. She looked at him, her lips parting to suggest that they continue their conversation indoors, but he was talking brusquely and she could not interrupt.

'You will have to take them back, because they can't stay here.' It was not an argument; he left no room for negotiation or discussion. His long, black-gloved hand made a chopping movement sideways, symbolically ending their exchange, and he turned towards the *château* in a curt movement.

Christabel caught hold of his arm. 'Look, Monsieur de Bellème——'

His black head swung, he stared down pointedly at her hand. *'Je vous en prie...'* I beg you, he said, meaning please take your hand off me, and his voice was so arrogant that she flushed, teeth meeting, and did not remove her hand, realising that if she did he would immediately walk off and leave her and the children stranded out here in the fierce, howling wind, in the night, with miles to walk before they got back to the little town below.

*'Monsieur,* we have nowhere to go tonight!'

'There is a hotel in town, they will have plenty of rooms.'

'How are we to get there?'

'How did you get here?' The sarcasm was icy; she tried to answer as coldly, but her indignation burned in her voice.

'We came by taxi and the driver left us here.'

Nina was crying, her face buried in Christabel's hip, and Christabel automatically stroked the child's soft fair hair, her hand rhythmic, soothing. Roland de Bellème glanced down at the little girl, at the stroking, caressing hand.

'And it is eleven o'clock now,' Christabel said angrily. 'By the time we got back to the hotel it would probably be midnight, and from the look of that town everyone will be in bed and fast asleep and we would not be given rooms until morning.'

He grimaced wryly. 'You're probably right. They keep early hours, and they wouldn't approve of such a young woman turning up out of the blue with two children in the middle of the night. Like me, they would probably just tell you to go away.'

'What do you suggest we do for the rest of the night? Sleep on the beach?' Christabel muttered, glowering at him.

'Don't try to make me feel guilty over your predicament, *mademoiselle*! I didn't invite you. Far from it, I made it crystal-clear that I did not want visitors, and I am not responsible for what becomes of you now that my sister-in-law has chosen to ignore what I said to her.'

Dani scowled at him, her small face dark red with sudden temper. 'Don't you shout at Bel! You're a bad man, and I don't like you.'

'Dani!' Christabel hurriedly said, shaking her head. 'You must not talk to your uncle like that.'

'He talks to you like that!'

'Just because someone else is bad-mannered, it does not mean you have *carte blanche* to be rude yourself!' Christabel looked up a little defiantly, and met Roland de Bellème's narrowed eyes. '*Monsieur*, can we go inside out of this wind?' she asked coolly. 'The children and I are cold. We have been travelling all day, from Paris, it is very late, and we are tired. Surely you have one spare room we could use for tonight?'

His brows met and he tilted his head to inspect her face, those disturbing dark eyes half hidden by heavy lids which he had lowered as if to hide his thoughts from her. She could not tell from his sharply planed, olive-skinned face what he was thinking, either. His face kept its secrets.

'Are you their nurse? An English nanny, I suppose? Your French is not bad, but you still have a distinct accent that gives you away.' From his tone she gathered that her nationality was not in her favour, which did not surprise her. She had been in France long enough to discover the depth of the national prejudice against their neighbours; a prejudice reflected from the other side of the channel by the English, of course! The two nations were like an old married couple, needing each other and yet always quarrelling over trifles.

'I'm a student, actually, working for a degree in French literature and art at the Sorbonne. I live with your sister-in-law during my term times, and work for her as an *au pair* whenever I am free from lectures. I look after the children while I study, and

I also cook meals and clean the apartment. I'm not a trained nanny or children's nurse. I just like children.'

He studied her curiously, watching her stroking Nina's hair. 'I see that they like you, too.'

She went a little pink. 'Children, like animals, always like anyone who is kind to them.'

He laughed shortly and pulled on his dog's ears. 'Caesar is not that easy to tame, I warn you, so don't imagine you'll get round him with your little pats and smiles.' There was an icy irony in his stare that gave her an idea that he was not just talking about his dog. Did he really imagine she would be stupid enough to try flirting with him? Her flush deepened and she glared at him.

'Don't worry, Caesar is safe from me!' She hoped he realised she meant that Caesar's master was safe from her, too.

He stared at her with raised brows and a curling smile of mockery. 'Very well. You can all stay tonight. For one night only! In the morning you must all return to Paris.'

He turned on his heel and led the way into the *château*, unlocking the massive iron-studded gate which creaked open, making Nina jump, her little face apprehensive. Dani looked furtively up at Christabel.

'We can't go back home, though, can we?' she whispered. '*Maman* isn't there.'

Christabel put a finger over her mouth, shaking her head. 'Don't say anything yet,' she whispered back and Dani gave a nervous little giggle.

The great hound had padded past its master and was vanishing into the *château*. Roland de Bellème looked back at Christabel.

'What's all the whispering about? Are you coming in or not? I don't want the whole place full of cold night air.'

She and the two little girls walked past into a high-vaulted, shadowy hall, the walls hung with ancient, but highly polished armour: swords, daggers, shields, arranged in formal patterns against white-washed stone.

A leaping flicker of firelight played among the weapons, made black shadows on the ceiling. A fire of great logs burnt on a stone hearth, the flames licking up into the ancient, smoke-blackened chimney, blue and green and orange flames which spat and crackled out of the well-dried applewood which gave off a delicious fragrance, the incense of summer orchards long vanished.

Caesar had already found a place at the hearth; he lay in front of the fire with his nose on his paws, his drooping eyelids leaving just a watchful slit so that he could observe the strangers in his home.

'Oh, a fire!' Dani said, running over to hold out her hands to the warmth and light, her fear of the dog quite forgotten in her enchantment at finding a log fire burning in the hall. Nina clung on to Christabel a moment longer, then crept over to join her sister. The two children stared, hypnotised, into the depths of the flames.

'What are their names?' Roland de Bellème asked, and Christabel looked up at him incredulously. He must surely remember the names of his own nieces? If he did not, what sort of man was he?

Eve-Marie had several times talked to her about her dead husband, so she knew something of the family history. There had been no other children in the family, and the Bellème parents had died many years ago, leaving Roland and Hilaire de Bellème, neither of them yet twenty, alone in the decaying splendour of their home. Hilaire had hated it in the country; he had gone off to Paris and had plunged into the life of the city with eager excitement. He had had a number of jobs, at none of which was he very successful. Roland had been at an agricultural college when his parents died. While he was there, he had joined the amateur drama group, and had become obsessed with drama. After he had qualified, he had come back here to the *château* to farm the family land. That had not been enough for him, though. A few years later he had written a play, and it had been performed and become a huge success overnight. Hilaire was acting, too, by then. He had met and married Eve-Marie, and they had been expecting their first baby during the year when Roland de Bellème's first play was put on in Paris.

How could he forget a year full of such exciting events? Or forget the name of the child born that year?

'Danielle and Nina,' she said reproachfully, and he watched the two little girls with an unreadable expression on his face.

'I don't see anything of my brother in them. They're the image of their mother,' he said in an odd voice, frowning, and Christabel wondered if that made him hostile towards the children. Was that why he hadn't wanted to have them here? He must have loved his brother, who had been three years younger. Hilaire's death must have been a traumatic shock, especially when it had been so shortly followed by the death of Roland de Bellème's wife. No wonder he had retreated back here to the *château* and stopped writing. Eve-Marie hadn't talked about Roland's wife, but Roland must have loved her passionately to be so broken by her death.

'Well?' his deep voice asked impatiently, and she broke out of her reverie to realise he had asked her a question. Dazedly, she turned her amber eyes on him, their black pupils dilated, and Roland stared into them.

'I'm sorry, what did you say?' she faltered.

'Have you eaten? If so, shouldn't the children go to bed?' he repeated in a dry voice as her pale face drowned in a flood of colour.

'Oh, yes, yes, we ate on the train. And the children are exhausted, they must get to bed. If you'll show us to a room...I'm happy to share with them. They'll feel better if I'm there, in a strange room, anyway. Children find new surroundings disorientating at first, and need something familiar around them to make them feel at home——'

'I don't want them to start feeling at home!' he interrupted brusquely. 'They—and you—return to Paris tomorrow.'

Christabel lifted her head and his dark eyes followed the defiant little movement with narrowed wariness. All she said, though, was, 'If you'll show us to this room, then.' She called the children, who came slowly, yawning, their faces now pink from the heat of the fire, their eyes drowsy. She put an arm round each and Roland de Bellème gestured towards the sweeping staircase leading out of the great hall up to the first floor, where they could see ancient panelling on the walls.

'This must be much later than the hall,' Christabel said, touching the panelling with a caressing hand as they walked along the balustraded landing. 'It looks sixteenth century.'

The wood was highly polished; someone had taken great care of it over the years. Roland threw open a door at the far end of the landing. 'This room should do for the children.' They slowly went into the room, which had been furnished simply in shades of green and white—green curtains, and matching coverlets on the beds, parquet floors strewn with woven wool rugs of striped green and white, and gloss-painted white walls on which hung modern paintings of spring landscapes. Christabel did not recognise the artist, but they were charming, and so was the room. The children exclaimed in delight over it before they began to argue over who should have which of the two beds.

Christabel's eyes were shrewd as she glanced around, very struck by the décor. She did not believe Roland de Bellème was responsible for the immaculate condition of the house. Despite what he said, there must be a woman somewhere.

Before the children came to blows, however, she intervened to point out that they would be sharing one bed while she slept in the other, since the room only contained two beds.

'There is a room next door for you,' Roland de Bellème drily contradicted, and walked over to a door she had not noticed, threw it open and let her see the room beyond, which was smaller, furnished in Victorian style, with floral-sprigged wallpaper, and heavy mahogany bed, wardrobe and chest of drawers. The bed was covered with dark red velvet; curtains of the same material hung at the windows. It was a gloomy little room, and the expression on Roland de Bellème's face made it clear that he read Christabel's reaction all too easily, and was amused by it.

'Isn't it good enough for you?' he mocked, and she turned to outface him.

'It looks very comfortable, and I could sleep on anything tonight.' She glanced at her watch. 'So, if you don't mind, we'll all get to bed.' She walked back to the children and told them to get undressed and wash briefly at the washbasin in their bedroom while she went back downstairs to get the cases.

Roland walked out of the room ahead of her. 'I'll get the cases,' he said over his shoulder, returning with them a moment later, carrying them easily as if they weighed no more than a feather, to her fury.

He put them down on the end of one of the beds, and turned to go. 'Goodnight, *monsieur*,' Christabel said, nudging Dani, who chimed in,

'Goodnight, Uncle Roland.' She gave her little sister a commanding nod and Nina shyly said it, too.

Roland de Bellème turned, his black eyes hard. Christabel stiffened at the look on his face, then he nodded to the children.

'Goodnight.' He didn't leave then, however. He threw Christabel a look, his face harsh. 'When you've put them to bed, come downstairs. I want to talk to you.'

'I'm very tired, *monsieur*. Can't it wait till morning——?'

'No.' He shut the door with a little snap and she heard his rapid, angry footsteps departing along the landing. Christabel stood listening for a moment until she heard the two little girls squabbling over who was to use the washbasin first, so she ran to separate them and tell Dani to let Nina have first turn tonight so that she could get to bed faster.

'Help me find your nighties,' she said to Dani, who was looking sulky. They were both overtired by now, barely able to keep their eyes open. Five minutes later they were both tucked up in bed, and Christabel kissed them affectionately before turning out the light.

'You've been very good girls all day. I'll tell your *maman* how good you've been when I write to her tomorrow.'

Dani yawned so wide that her face seemed to be all mouth. 'Will you take us with you to England, now, Bel? I'd like that.'

Christabel vaguely said, 'We'll see. Go to sleep now.' She closed the door and walked as quietly as she could down the landing. The end of it closest to the stairs formed a sort of minstrel's gallery, with a beautifully carved balustrade running along the top of the stairs so that you could see from there down into the great hall. Christabel paused to lean over, getting a different view of the white walls and cross-beamed ceiling, the enormous stone fireplace large enough for a man to sit inside, the flagged floor on which were laid faded oriental rugs, the play of firelight on very old, highly polished furniture, and above all a new angle on the owner of all this, Roland de Bellème. He was sitting in a high-backed tapestry-covered chair, black-booted feet stretched out towards the fire, his face in profile to her, sharply lit by the leaping fire.

She stared down at him, wondering what he was thinking about, her curiosity about him in no way assuaged by having actually met him. But then it would be conceited to imagine that in such a short time she could discover what made him tick. The man who had written that strange, disturbing play was unlikely to be so easily understood.

He had raised too many questions in the play which he never answered, for one thing, and for another, Christabel's head rang with questions about his own life, too.

Why had he stopped writing, for instance? Why did he never go to the theatre any more, even to see his own plays? Why did he never go to Paris or meet any of his old friends, and why, when they came down here to Brittany, did he refuse to see them, even if they called at the *manoir*?

That, at least, was what Eve-Marie had told her once, and she had had no motive for lying as far as Christabel knew. It had been the most casual of conversations; the revelations about Roland had come out in a very haphazard way, and Eve-Marie had shown no sign of malice or dislike of him. On the contrary, Christabel had picked up sympathy in her, almost a sadness, perhaps because they had both lost the one they loved.

He wasn't quite as she had expected, either. Eve-Marie had said that he was in his late thirties; she had called him a recluse, which was obviously true, but she had not mentioned Roland's dark good looks or that disturbing sexuality.

Christabel bit her lip, her face beginning to burn. Why on earth had she thought that?

OK, he was very much a man, and he made her feel very aware of being a woman, and all without making any overt move or remark. The arrogant glance of those dark eyes, the physical power of his body, had a worrying effect on her senses. She couldn't remember ever feeling this way before, and it alarmed her. Her friends at the Sorbonne would be alarmed, too; they would violently disapprove if they knew how she'd reacted to him. All that macho masculinity was utterly out of fashion with girls of her age. Equality was what they were after, and Christabel's head agreed one hundred per cent with them. Unfortunately, it wasn't her mind that was so intensely aware of Roland de Bellème, it was other parts of her over which she apparently had little mental control.

Suddenly his deep voice made her jump. 'Are you going to stand there all night? Come down!'

He hadn't moved or looked round, she hadn't knowingly made a sound—how had he known she was there? Very flushed, she reluctantly began to walk down the sweeping staircase, thinking that she was wrongly dressed—she should be wearing a crinoline, or skirts held high by a farthingale, so that she swished and rustled on every stair. Modern clothes were so boring.

She reached the hall and crossed to the fireplace, a nervous pulse beating in her throat.

'What did you want to talk to me about?' she huskily began as she reached him, but without answering he gestured with one hand for her to move nearer the fire so that he could see her face without himself needing to move.

She had obeyed before she had worked that out, then she glowered resentfully at him. He was treating her as if she were a servant! Did he still believe she was a nanny, in spite of her denial?

'Look, Monsieur de Bellème, I'm very tired and I want to get some sleep, so could you say what you have to say and then let me go back upstairs?'

He was drinking a glass of red wine, taking a sip and then holding it up to stare at the firelight glinting through it. He slowly turned those harsh black eyes on her, ran a glance from her brown head to her feet, his lip curling in silent comment on what he saw. She knew she wasn't beautiful— not even pretty, come to that—but her stomach churned with bitter affront at the way in which he was eying her. She felt like turning round and walking away, but he spoke before she could.

'I overheard something one of the children was whispering,' he said bitingly. 'Where is my sister-in-law?'

Christabel hesitated, afraid to tell him the truth.

'Where is she?' he snarled.

'She's...' Christabel was so jumpy her voice shook, and that made her angry. If he was going to bully her anyway, she might as well give him something to snap about. Taking a deep breath, she told him the truth. 'She's on her way to Martinique.'

She saw his strong brown hand tighten on the stem of the wine-glass; his knuckles showed white. 'Damn her!' he ground out between clenched teeth. 'She's actually on her way? How? By air or——'

'Air.'

'When did she leave?'

'This morning.'

'After sending her children off with you on the train to Brittany, I suppose! She thought I couldn't do anything about it if she sent them and then disappeared to the other side of the world, did she? *Fait accompli*, in other words! Well, she is going to find she's very mistaken if she thinks she can trick me like this. I am not having her children foisted on to me, and that's final. You can take them back to the Paris apartment and look after them there until she gets back.' He lifted his glass and drained the contents, his brown throat moving in a long swallow while she stared at him.

'I can't,' she said flatly.

He frowned, putting down his wine-glass. 'What?'

'I began my summer vacation yesterday, in fact. I should be home in England now, but Madame de Bellème asked me to bring the children here to you first. My family expect me back by the ferry tomorrow.'

He got to his feet in an abrupt movement that sent her stumbling backwards away from him.

'You can ring them and tell them the arrangements have been changed! I'll pay you well to take care of the children. Name your own price, I don't care how much it costs—I cannot have them here. You must take them back home to Paris.'

Christabel watched him warily, afraid his reaction to what she was going to tell him would be even more explosive. 'I can't take them back to Paris, *monsieur*. Madame de Bellème let her flat to some German tourists for a month.'

He swore violently, moving with restless fury. 'So that's it? She rang me up and gave me all that sentimental stuff about family, about her children needing to know they had an uncle and how they ought to get to know the *manoir* because of all their ancestors . . . and all the time her motive was actually money!'

'Oh, I don't think you can say that!' protested Christabel, and he swung to glare at her, his eyes like the rage-flecked eyes of his great black hound that evening as it had rushed at her out of the darkness.

'She wanted to let her apartment and earn some extra cash, and to do that she had to push her children on to someone else, so I was chosen for the honour!'

'She would have taken the children with her, but she had forgotten to have their passports renewed and it was too late to get them before she had to leave for Martinique!'

'How convenient!' he sneered. 'Well, I am not going to let her get away with her neat little plan. You can take them to England with you.'

'I can't——'

'You will have to! You can't leave them here!'

'And I can't take them to England because they don't have—— '

'Passports,' he heavily finished for her, grimacing. 'Damn it to hell . . . well, then, you must take them to a hotel somewhere, have a seaside holiday with them at my expense. I'll find you a luxury hotel, where you can live like a princess for a month, until Eve-Marie comes back.'

Christabel had a sneaking sympathy with him; it was obvious that he wasn't the sort of man who enjoyed looking after little children, and no doubt the arrival of his nieces would disrupt his normally peaceful existence, but this was his problem, not hers. She was not shouldering all the responsibility for the little girls, however much he paid her. He had no idea how tiring they could be if you were in sole charge of them for twenty-four hours a day. She was fond of them, and she quite enjoyed looking after them for a while, but she had had enough for the moment. She needed a break from the children and the work in the apartment. Next year was her final year, graduation examinations loomed, and she knew she would have to spend a lot of the summer in revising and working hard at her studies. She couldn't spare the energy to look after the children, too.

'I'm sorry, *monsieur*,' she said, her face stubborn. 'I cannot possibly give up a whole month to looking after your nieces. I have to work hard this summer, for my final exams. I wouldn't have time to work if I had the children with me all the time.'

He made a rough, angry noise in his throat, picked up his empty wine-glass and prowled away with it, refilling it from a bottle from an antique cabinet against the wall. Over his shoulder he asked, 'Some wine?'

'No, thank you. I must go to bed,' Christabel politely said, hoping that at last he realised how matters stood.

'Not yet,' he said, coming back, the glass in his hand. He made that peremptory gesture again, silently ordering her to sit down on a three-legged wooden stool beside the hearth. She stood her ground, lifting her brows, and he scowled. 'You can spare me another half-hour, surely? You can't be that tired.'

'You might try asking me to sit down instead of just waving your hand in that overbearing fashion!'

'Oh, might I?' He considered her, drank some more wine, then considered her again while she grew more flushed and more angry. 'Oh, I can see why Eve-Marie picked you to move into her apartment,' he finally said. 'You're a typical Englishwoman— plain and blunt, that's how you love to describe yourselves, isn't it? And what you mean is that you don't intend to be diplomatic, and you know you're no beauty——'

'Thank you!' she snapped, dark red and furious.

'You'd be no threat to Eve-Marie,' he finished, and drained his glass once more, smiling drily at her angry expression. 'My dear sister-in-law is typical of her sex. She prefers other women not to be as lovely, or as clever, or as successful with men as she is herself!'

'Goodnight, *monsieur*!' Christabel wasn't listening to any more of this. She headed for the stairs, but Roland de Bellème caught up with her before she had got very far. He was laughing, his dark eyes icily mocking as he grabbed her by the arms.

'Did I wound your vanity, *mademoiselle*? I'm sorry—how can I make amends? Shall I kiss it better?'

She turned rigid in his grip, her face suddenly pale, although oddly her blood was crashing through her veins like the surf pounding the rocks on the beach below this house. How much wine had he drunk before she came down? He had to be drunk, if not crazy! She felt dizzy. It was shock, her blood-pressure must be heading for the stratosphere!

'Let go of me, *monsieur*. This isn't funny... I... you can't...'

'Who can't?' he murmured, pulling her towards him, his thigh against her leg. 'I'll teach you to come here uninvited, force your way into my home... what do you think happens to girls who act like that? You were gambling that I'd behave like a gentleman, were you? And what if I don't? Or what if gentlemen have learnt to be more ruthless, to take what's offered without looking too closely at it?'

'Stop talking to me like that!' she burst out angrily.

'Oh, do you want me to pretend you're pretty, that you've turned my head? You're a woman, that's all that matters at the moment.' He dragged her towards him, ignoring her struggles, and stifled her protests with the suffocating force of his mouth.

The minute she had first seen him, out in the dark night, she had known instinctively that he could be brutal and arrogant. For a flash of time she had almost believed she was seeing some throwback to his ancestors—the master of this ancient house striding to confront intruders, as no doubt he would have done centuries ago, his hound running at his side. Then she had laughed at herself for letting such a fantasy take hold of her, because Roland de Bellème was very much a man of today; he was no dream of yesterday.

Now, though, as his hard mouth forced her lips apart, his tongue hotly thrusting between them, an atavistic fear took hold of her again. She was a slightly built girl, lacking the physical strength to fight; she struggled uselessly in his hands. It was humiliating not to be able to stop him, but far more humiliating to know deep inside herself that even as she writhed and fought she was violently aware of his body, of the grace and power of it as it controlled her with all the arrogant allure of the bullfighter tormenting a bull. Christabel shocked herself by the drag of her senses towards him. He was practically a stranger; she didn't know or like him. How could she possibly want to kiss him back, touch him, make love with him?

She could not feel like that! It was crazy, impossible. It must be an illusion brought on by exhaustion and these strange surroundings. She kicked his ankle as hard as she could, in the end, and he swore thickly, lifting his head, his face darkly flushed, his eyes brilliant.

'I haven't had a woman for longer than I like to remember,' he said hoarsely. 'You made a dangerous mistake, coming here tonight, English girl.'

Shock hit her like a tidal wave. He was still holding her by the upper arms, his long fingers hurting. Christabel watched him with worried eyes. He couldn't mean what he seemed to mean! Oh, God, what had she got herself into? It hadn't entered her head until now that she had been taking any risks in coming to a strange house, staying here alone with a strange man. She had been looking after his dead brother's children for two years. She had felt like part of his family. It hadn't even occurred to her that Roland de Bellème might try to seduce her or, worse, rape her.

'I'll be leaving tomorrow!' she shakily said. 'And if you lay one finger on me, I'll . . . I'll see you pay for it!'

He laughed at her. 'Oh, I'm really frightened,' he mocked, eyes sheathed in ice, yet on fire, too, with a bitter desire that was far from a compliment, that felt like the threat of an enemy.

'You're crazy!' she burst out, or was that unwise? Should you tell a madman that he was crazy? 'Or drunk!' she hurriedly added, and he laughed again.

'You think I'd have to be drunk to want to make love to you?'

She flinched, her amber eyes filled with hurt. How could he be so brutal to someone he hardly knew? She hadn't done anything to him! Then she thought with even more shock and pain...what has happened to this man to make him like this?

She looked at him in silence then, angrily sorry for him, shaken to her roots, and he observed her white face, his mouth twisting.

'What was it the children called you? Bel? Well, not a name that fits, but in the dark all cats are grey. Your body isn't at all bad, as far as I can judge under those terrible clothes—why do Englishwomen wear such terrible clothes? Well, who cares? Who cares what your face looks like? I need to bury myself in a woman's body tonight— I don't give a damn whether she's pretty or not!'

# CHAPTER THREE

CHRISTABEL was too frightened to move or speak
for what seemed an eternity, and while she stared
up at him, her eyes all black, glazed pupil, her face
a dead white, Roland de Bellème stared back at her
as if minutely observing her reactions.

Suddenly, he threw her away with a gesture like
disgust—whether for her or for himself she couldn't
tell. 'Oh, get upstairs, go to bed,' he snarled.
'You're safe from me, you little schoolgirl!'

She ran, sobbing, shaking, not feeling safe until
she was in the gloomy little bedroom with the doors
on each side bolted. She knew she wouldn't sleep
now; she wouldn't feel safe enough to relax. If one
of the children wanted her, she would hear them
before they tried her door.

She sank on the bed, wrapping her arms around
herself, and rocked backwards and forwards, face
tear-stained, her head rioting with questions and
worries. He was the strangest man she had ever met.
He was certainly dangerous—was he crazy? Or had
he merely drunk too much tonight? Wine wasn't as
potent as spirits, she had always gathered, but
perhaps it could have quite a powerful effect if you
drank enough of it! That strange play had given a
glimpse into his mind; it should have warned her,
but you didn't imagine that a writer was really like
his work, did you?

She was cold, so she undressed and put on a long cotton nightdress and a dressing-gown, tied the belt tightly around her waist, then climbed into her bed. She had found a book in her overnight bag and made herself read, leaning back on a pile of snowy-white pillows; but despite her nervousness her lids were heavy and she was very tired. She kept drifting off, eyes closing, then waking with a jerk. The book dropped from her hands; she slept.

She was woken by loud knocking on the door between her room and that of the children. Dazed and half asleep, she threw back the covers and stumbled to open it, only then realising that it was morning. Daylight filled the charming white and green room, showing her Dani and Nina with excited faces, their hands grabbing hers.

'Come and see, Bel...horses!' said Dani.

Nina gabbled, 'Lots of them, in the meadow outside. Look out of this window—aren't they marvellous?'

Still drowsy, Christabel let them pull her across their room to one of the two windows. Last night both had been shuttered; this morning the shutters had been folded back, giving a clear view of the *château* surroundings. In the dark, from the front, she had only seen trees around the *château*, a windbreak of pine and thorn trees. This bedroom was on the side of the building, however; from this window you could see a rough parkland, unmown wild grass rustling and tossing in the wind, and, grazing on it, half-a-dozen horses.

'Do you think our uncle will let us ride them?' Dani asked eagerly.

'I want to ride the brown one,' Nina said, her face dreamy.

'Oh, no! The white one is the best,' Dani argued, then considered the favoured horse, her head on one side in a very adult way. 'Well, greyish, I suppose. He looks like a rocking-horse, doesn't he? All dapply, grey and white. He's lovely.'

'Do you think uncle will let us ride them?' Nina asked Christabel, who was yawning.

'Sorry... I didn't sleep well last night. I don't know what your uncle is likely to say, but he can only say either yes or no, so I should just ask him and see what happens.' Christabel turned away, and Dani slipped a hand into hers.

'You ride horses at home in England, don't you, Bel? I remember you told us about your horse, Custard.'

Both little girls began to giggle. 'Custard...' Nina chuckled.

'Custard wasn't my horse, he belonged to a neighbour who let me ride him!'

'It's such a funny name. Why was he called Custard?'

'Because his mother was called Cherry Pie.'

The little girls looked blank, and Christabel made a wry face, realising that not being English they did not get the joke. 'In England, we serve custard— it's a hot sauce, made of milk—over fruit pies. So when Cherry Pie had a foal, they called him Custard.'

Dani laughed politely; Nina still looked blank. 'But will you ride with us, Bel?' asked Dani, and Christabel sighed, hoping that she was not going to have a problem making them understand what she was going to say.

'I won't be here, remember, Dani? I'm going back to England now that I've delivered you to your uncle.'

'Don't leave us!' Nina burst out, throwing herself at Christabel, clinging with both hands and feet to her, like a baby monkey to its mother. Christabel stroked her hair, feeling guilty and angry all at the same time. Eve-Marie should not have done this to her! It was unfair to land her with the responsibility for these children. Their mother should have brought them here.

'I don't like Uncle Roland,' Dani said, more grown-up than her sister, but her lower lip trembling. 'He's scary.'

'He's a monster,' Nina wailed, clinging harder.

'Now, stop it! You're just working yourselves up into a silly state over nothing,' Christabel said firmly, detaching Nina and bending to look into her face. 'Your uncle will be very kind to you, and you'll have lots of fun. I'm sure he'll let you ride the horses, and you can explore the *château*, and go down to the beach to swim, and I'm sure he'll take you into town to eat ice-cream. Oh, there will be lots to do, you're going to love it here.'

They looked obstinately unconvinced, their small faces sulky. 'Why can't you stay? Who's going to look after us, help us get dressed, play with us?' asked Dani, and Christabel heaved another sigh. She was very fond of the two little girls. It was going to be very difficult to walk away from them, leaving them here with that man. He was no fit person to look after two small children; in her opinion their mother shouldn't have sent them here. Didn't she know what sort of man Roland de Bellème was?

'Get dressed,' she said, deciding to shelve the matter for the moment. She would have to go into town today to check on train times and buy a ticket for the ferry to England. As she wasn't taking a car she was sure she would have no difficulty booking a passage on the ferry, so she had left that until now, but then she had not anticipated having so much trouble with Roland de Bellème. She had imagined blithely that she would deliver the children to him and spend a night in town at a hotel before taking a train to Brest to get the ferry. Brest was an hour away, by train, she had estimated after studying the map. In Paris it had all seemed so uncomplicated! How could she have guessed her optimistic plans would all go wrong?

'You won't go away without telling us, will you?' pleaded Nina, watching her with suspicion, and Christabel shook her head ruefully. She had already realised that she had to stay for a short while, at least, to make quite sure that the children had settled down and were going to be well looked after. There had to be a woman here, somewhere. It had not been Roland de Bellème who did the housework, kept this place so immaculate, had made up these beds, polished the panelling, cleaned all these windows. It must be a full-time job; the *manoir* was so big, and to any woman's eye it was clear that it had been lovingly cared for and cleaned. If Roland could afford to pay a woman to look after his home, he could pay someone to look after the children.

'Come on, let's find the bathroom,' Christabel told them cheerfully.

'We already did,' said Nina, opening her eyes wide, and Christabel laughed.

'I know we did, silly! I meant let's go and run your baths.'

'You said find the bathroom,' argued Nina, and Dani pushed her.

'Shut up, stupid!'

'You shut up!' Nina pushed her back.

'Stop that!' Christabel said firmly, taking a faintly nervous glance down the landing. 'We don't want to wake your uncle, do we?'

'Does he sleep late, like *Maman*?' asked Nina, not surprised by the idea, since her mother kept theatrical hours, going to bed late after a show and getting up late in the morning, often around lunchtime.

'I don't know, but if he isn't up we don't want to disturb him, do we?' Christabel said, pushing them both into the bathroom across the corridor. She turned on the taps, relieved to find hot water gushing out of one. Well, that was one of her worries disposed of—the place did have plenty of hot water! There were interesting large glass dome-topped jars on the window-sill; some held coloured bath-salts, others held tiny pieces of soap in different colours, shaped as flowers, hearts, birds, all manner of objects. Christabel let Dani choose her own bath-salts; a shower of lavender fell into the steaming water and a delicious fragrance rose into the air.

Christabel added more cold water until the bath was at the right temperature. The two little girls were arguing over which soap they wanted; Nina chose a white dove, Dani chose a pink rose. They were going to take their bath together to save time, so they pulled their nighties over their heads and climbed into the large, white-enamelled Victorian tub, splashing and giggling.

'Now, be good, don't splash water over the side of the bath. I'll be back in five minutes,' Christabel said, leaving them.

She paused in the corridor again, listening for any indication that Roland de Bellème was up, but the only sounds she could hear were the chatter and laughter of the little girls.

Well, in all probability Roland hadn't been able to get himself out of bed this morning. He must have a hangover! Had he stopped drinking after she'd left, or had he sat down there for another hour or so, pouring wine down his throat? It wouldn't surprise her to know that he had fallen into bed last night dead drunk.

How often did he drink like that? She went into her bedroom and chose the clothes she would wear that day, her brow furrowed.

How could she possibly leave the children with him? Her imagination ran riot, envisaging all sorts of terrifying situations. What if he got drunk one night and burnt this place down? Oh, that was absurd... he wouldn't do that. But what if Nina woke up in the middle of the night, with a nightmare, and he blundered in here, in a drunken condition... She groaned, standing still, her eyes aghast, picturing it.

How could she go off home for a holiday, knowing that the little girls were here alone with this man? She would never be able to enjoy herself;

she would constantly be worrying, imagining the worst, and if anything did happen she would blame herself. Of course, she wasn't their mother, and Eve-Marie had apparently been quite happy to leave her children with him, but Christabel was the adult responsible for them now, and she was far less complacent about it.

She shook herself crossly. She would make a decision later today; first she would insist that Roland de Bellème must agree to pay someone else to take care of the children once she had left, and she would arrange to meet the other woman, to make sure she was suitable.

Then she would take the children with her into the little town, find out about the times of ferries from Brest, and book her ticket to Brest and from there to England. Once that was settled, she could ring her family and arrange to be met. They knew she was coming across on the ferry, but not the exact details of her arrival.

She went back into the bathroom and got the children out of their bath—with some difficulty, since they were enjoying themselves—and helped them dress in cotton jeans and T-shirts; Dani in pink, Nina in yellow. With their blonde hair and blue eyes they perfectly suited pastel shades, and looked enchanting.

Christabel took them back into their bedroom and gave each a book to read while she went to have her bath. 'And don't leave this room while I'm gone!' she ordered, frowning at them to make sure they obeyed her. 'You can watch the horses, but don't open the window. You could fall out.' She looked at Dani. 'I'm leaving you in charge,

Dani. Make sure Nina doesn't do anything naughty.'

Dani looked smug. 'Yes, Bel.' She loved being left in charge of her sister, just as Nina hated it.

Christabel hurried back to take her bath, shaking rose-scented bath crystals into the water and using a rose soap, as Dani had. She didn't linger over it, relaxing and delightful though it was to lie back in the fragrant water letting her tensions seep away. She was afraid to leave the children for any length of time, so within ten minutes she was back with them, bathed and dressed, her brown hair damply curling on her temples.

She had put on a simple, candy-striped, pink on white cotton summer dress; her legs were bare, her feet pushed into soft white leather open-toed sandals. She wasn't wearing make-up. She had hesitated, then defiantly decided not to bother. She was still burning up over the insults she had taken from Roland de Bellème last night.

She didn't want him to imagine for one second that she was plastering herself with make-up in a pathetic attempt to make herself look any prettier to him. He needn't think she cared what he thought of the way she looked! She detested him; his opinions didn't matter a damn to her, and anyway, surfaces never mattered as much as what lay underneath.

When she got back to the children they were both leaning against the window watching the horses, their faces rapt. Christabel smiled before she called them. There was no doubt about what they would be doing while they were here! In Paris, of course, they had no opportunity to ride horses, although there were riding stables in the city, and any day of the week you could see smartly dressed men and women riding beautifully groomed horses along the sandy forest paths in the Bois de Boulogne. For Dani and Nina, however, riding lessons were out of the question. Maybe when they were older their mother might agree, but they would have to be chaperoned if they took lessons now, and neither she nor Christabel were free every week to accompany them to a riding stable for a couple of hours.

'Shall we go and have breakfast?' she asked, and the little girls hurried over to join her, gabbling excitedly about the horses.

They went downstairs without hearing or seeing anything of Roland de Bellème. Several doors led off the hall, but when they peeped into them they were all empty—one a panelled dining-room with a heavy oak dining-table dominating it, and hanging on the walls portraits of sombre eighteenth-century gentlemen in powdered wigs, another a splendid drawing-room with yellow brocade curtains, a magnificent chandelier, and stiffly upholstered furniture.

'Now, I wonder which way leads to the kitchen?' said Christabel.

'That way,' guessed Dani, pointing to a door at the far end of the great hall.

'Well, we have to start somewhere, why not there?'

They pushed open the high panelled door and found themselves in a narrow corridor and a very different ambience. Gone were the polished panels, the parquet flooring, the gold-framed portraits, the elegant furniture. They were in the servants' quarters; the floor was tiled black and white, the walls painted dark green.

Nina shivered, moving closer to Christabel. 'I don't like it.'

'Nor do I,' said Dani.

'It is rather grim,' Christabel agreed, pushing open a door, then closing it again as she saw that it was just a store-room. She opened another and sighed with relief. 'Ah, the kitchen at last!'

It was not a modernised kitchen, although it did contain an electric stove and a refrigerator, but it was surprisingly cheerful. The walls had once been painted buttercup-yellow, which had faded a little, but which this morning reflected back the sunlight from high sashed windows which looked out over the meadows. That meant that the kitchen must lie just under their bedrooms, she realised. The children rushed over to stare out at the horses again, while Christabel glanced into the fridge, making a face. Well, there was milk and cheese and eggs— that was something! She filled a saucepan with milk and put it on to boil.

'I wonder if your uncle is up, and where he has got to?' she asked the children, who didn't seem to care. They were too absorbed in the horses.

Christabel made their morning chocolate and, while exploring the rest of the kitchen, found some packets of breakfast cereal in a cupboard, one of which she knew the little girls liked. She sat them down at the kitchen table, put their bowls of chocolate in front of them, set out the cereal, told them to be good, to eat their breakfast without making a mess, and not to move from the table until she

came back, then went off in search of Roland de
Bellème.

This time she hunted through all the rooms;
noting that there was no sign either of Roland or
a telephone. Hadn't he said that his sister-in-law
had talked to him on the phone? In that case, where
was it? This was a very large building; it could be
anywhere. Was Roland still be in bed—or had he
gone off to buy newly baked croissants and bread?
She stood in the great hall, calling him. There was
no reply at first, then from upstairs she heard a
muffled sound—a groan or a snarl, she couldn't be
sure which. She went warily up the stairs, calling
again.

A voice growled from a door near the top of the
stairs. Christabel knocked; the voice within swore
in angry French, and her teeth met, a flush
mounting to her forehead. Yes, that was Roland
de Bellème! She looked at her watch. It was gone
ten o'clock. Surely he couldn't still be in bed?

'*Monsieur*, are you up?' she asked, knocking
again.

'No, damn you, go away!' he roared.

'*Monsieur*, I'm sorry, but I have to talk to you.'

'Can't hear, go away,' he answered, his voice
muffled again, as if he had put his head under his
covers.

She opened the door and stood there, not looking
into the room, her eyes lowered discreetly in case
they might see something she would rather they did
not see.

'*Monsieur*, I must go down into the town this
morning, and I cannot find the telephone you men-

tioned . . . I want to ring for a taxi to come and pick me up.'

Another groan from the direction of the bed. 'My God, my head! Woman, go away, I'm too ill to be bothered with you.'

Christabel's temper got out of hand and she forgot to avert her eyes. She took a furious step into the room, staring at the four-poster bed which dominated it and the mound of bedclothes which hid the occupant.

'You're not ill! You've got a hangover, that's what's wrong with you—and you richly deserve one. Maybe that will teach you not to drink so much.'

'If there's one thing I can't stand it's a preaching woman!' he said, sitting up in the bed and shocking her with the discovery that he was sleeping naked, his chest deeply tanned, gleaming golden-brown against the white pillows, the centre of it roughened by a wedge of curling black hairs which ran down his body until the sheets hid where it ended. Her fascinated, nervous gaze lifted hurriedly again and met his narrowed stare. She felt hot blood rushing up her face, and turned to flee.

Roland laughed. That stopped her in her tracks. She didn't turn round, but with her back to him asked icily, 'Where is the telephone, *monsieur*? Tell me that and I'll leave you to enjoy your hangover in peace. I just want to make arrangements to get back to England as soon as possible.'

'Taking those brats with you?'

'We've been through all that! I can't take them to England because they don't have passports. The children have to stay here with you. I'm sure you can find someone to come in and look after them for you. What about the woman who cleans your home? Wouldn't she——?'

'She's past looking after children,' he said drily. 'She's seventy this year, and she's been talking about retiring for months.'

Christabel was disappointed and sighed; she had pinned her hopes on whoever cleaned his house.

'Well, I'm certain there must be someone suitable who would come and take charge of them until their mother returns!'

She heard the creak of the bedsprings, the rustle of bedclothes, and tensed. He wasn't getting out of that bed, was he? Then she heard his voice, muffled again, thickened by a yawn. 'I'm going back to sleep, don't disturb me again.'

'But the phone... Where...?'

'Haven't got one,' he said, yawning loudly.

'But——'

'Go away, will you?'

'Look, *monsieur*, I insist, I must phone for a taxi!' she persisted, going back into the room and staring at the four-poster, the rumpled quilt hiding him. A furious bellow came from under the bedclothes.

'Damn you, woman!' He threw back the covers and she got a glimpse of his chest again, his bare thigh, a long, hair-darkened leg.

That was when Christabel left, slamming the door after her. She ran back downstairs so fast that she could hardly breathe when she reached the hall, and paused there, flushed and gasping for air, looking over her shoulder in a distracted way, half expecting to see Roland de Bellème on her heels. There was silence from the upper house, however, and she weakly sank down on the last step, fuming. He had done that deliberately! He had pretended to be getting out of bed naked, certain that that would make her run away—and she had been idiot enough to fall for it!

She gritted her teeth, furious with herself for being such a fool. Just you wait, Monsieur Roland de Bellème! she thought darkly. You won't think yourself so clever when you're left with Dani and Nina on your hands. There's nothing like a couple of small children to cut a man down to size. I'd love to be a fly on these walls then, to watch you trying to cope with them!

Then a qualm hit her again, and she bit her lip. But could she in all conscience leave the children alone with him? She didn't give a damn about Roland de Bellème—but she was anxious about the children, left here with a man like that!

That reminded her that she had to get back to the kitchen—heaven only knew what they had been up to in her absence.

When she got back to the kitchen, however, the children still sat at the table, although they had finished their breakfast, but they were no longer alone. A small, spare Frenchwoman was with them, her hair, once obviously raven-black but now silvering, tied back in a tight bun, an enveloping apron tied firmly around her waist.

She look round and Christabel hesitantly smiled. 'Oh, good morning! You must be the lady who keeps the *manoir* looking so beautiful! Monsieur de Bellème told me you would be coming in ... but he didn't tell me your name, *madame* ... ?'

'Normand, Jeanne Normand.' Dark eyes inspected her, a work-lined hand was offered, a slow smile which lit up the brown, weathered face.

'I'm Christabel Paget. A pleasure to meet you, *madame.*' They shook hands and Christabel murmured, 'I expect the children explained why we are here?'

Madame Normand shrugged her shoulders and made a wry face. 'They told me something about their *maman* going away, but I didn't understand...'

'Madame de Bellème was offered a part in a film, you see, and... well, I've been living *en famille* with them in Paris while I study at the Sorbonne——'

'The Sorbonne?' Madame Normand looked astonished, then smiled. 'But you are English?'

Christabel nodded. 'I'm studying French literature.'

'Your French is so good, though! I wondered if you might be half French?'

'A quarter,' admitted Christabel. 'I had a French grandmother... although she is dead now. She used to tell me French fairy-stories and sing me French nursery rhymes when I was little. I suppose that's why I grew up loving French literature.'

'What you learn as a little child you remember all your life,' agreed Madame Normand, nodding vigorously. 'And so you come to France to study our literature, and you lodged with Madame de Bellème?'

'It was a wonderful chance for me; living *en famille* I got my rent and food free, and I could study in the evenings while I babysat for Madame when she was working on the stage.'

'A wonderful arrangement for her, too, one sees!'
Madame Normand said with a dry cynicism, and
Christabel laughed.

'It worked out well for both of us, on the whole,
but I was only there during the university term. I
prefer to go home to England during the university
vacations, but, of course, that was inconvenient for
Madame, and this spring she persuaded me to stay
on in Paris to take care of the children, because she
could not make any other arrangement. So I told
her I really must go home to see my family this
summer vacation, then Madame was offered this
film part, and had to go to Martinique, and she let
her apartment in Paris to some foreigners, and
asked me if I would take the children to their uncle
in Brittany. So, here we are!'

'Why didn't she take them with her?'

Christabel explained about the lapsed passports
and Madame gave her another cynical look.

'And so you are not going to get home this
summer? That is a pity. Your parents will be upset?'

'Oh, I am still going! I just brought the children
down here, I'm not staying.'

'You mean, you are going to England now,
leaving them here?' Madame Normand looked
worried, a frown wrinkling her brown forehead.
'With Monsieur? Does their mother know what she
is doing? I do not say that Monsieur would ill-treat
them, but he has never looked after children in his
life. He won't know what to do, and this is no house
for little girls, anyway. If they were boys, and a
year or two older, maybe! He would let a boy run
wild, and no harm would come to him. A boy could
go out with Monsieur Roland ... you know, most

days he is out, riding, working with the men on the land. And while he's out there will be nobody here to watch the children. Madame de Bellème must be crazy, sending them to him!'

'I suppose...you...couldn't...?' Christabel hesitated and the old woman laughed shortly, shaking her head.

'Me? Heavens, no! I am too old to be running after little children. I have seven grandchildren, and having just one of them in the house for an hour leaves me feeling worn out. No, no, I could not take on the full-time responsibility for these two.'

'They aren't any trouble!' Christabel rather desperately assured her.

Madame Normand gave them a sideways smile. 'I'm sure they are very good girls, one can see they are! Blonde and sweet, like their dear mother! Oh, yes, I remember her well from when Monsieur Hilaire...' She crossed herself and sighed. 'God rest him. He brought her here many times when they were first married.' She sighed again, looking out of the window, her dark eyes fixed in thought, a melancholy expression on her face. 'Such folly...ah, but it was not Monsieur Hilaire's fault...some women are like cats, all silky fur and purring, until suddenly the claws come out.'

Christabel was bewildered; what on earth was she talking about? Surely not Eve-Marie? She gave the children a sideways glance, anxiety in her amber eyes. She hoped Madame Normand would not talk about their mother in front of them!

Giving herself a little shake, the old woman broke out of her reverie and briskly said, 'But that's all over! Forgotten! Now, mademoiselle, have you had breakfast?'

'Not yet. I was just going to make myself some coffee.'

'It is made!'

Christabel laughed, realising then that she could smell it—the morning smell of France, the best coffee in the world, strong, delicious, waking you up with a vengeance. There was another scent in the kitchen, too, now that she took time to notice it. She looked around and saw the crisp stick of bread on the breadboard, a basket of croissants beside it.

'Oh, marvellous! You brought some bread and croissants!'

Madame Normand nodded. 'I cycle past the bakery on my way here, so I pick up the morning bread. The first thing I do when I arrive each day is make the coffee. Monsieur Roland is up with the lark every day. He just has his first cup of coffee before he goes out, milking the cows with Gaston, the cowman, or starting on the day's chores else-where on the farm, but he always comes back at ten o'clock to take his coffee and croissants while he reads his newspaper, which I also pick up on my way here.' She frowned at the old farmhouse kitchen clock which ticked ponderously on the wall. 'It is half-past ten! He is late today.'

'He is still in bed,' Christabel said drily, and Madame Normand looked at her with incredulity.

'At this hour? He must be ill! What is wrong with him?'

Christabel was surprised by her reaction. So it was not normal for Roland de Bellème to get drunk and stay in bed the next morning? Maybe she had misjudged him?

'He has a hangover, I'm afraid,' she said in a low voice, hoping not to attract the children's attention. They were back at the window, gazing worshipfully at the horses once more.

'You're not serious?' Madame Normand was open-mouthed, staring at her.

'I'm afraid it's true. He was drinking wine last night, very late, and this morning he has a headache and refuses to get up.'

Madame Normand threw another sidelong look at the children, lowering her own voice. 'No doubt he could not face the idea of having them here! He isn't the most patient man in the world, and he is used to his own company. He spends most days alone, unless he is working with Gaston, or Jacques, who comes two days a week to do odd jobs.' She picked up the bread and chopped it into pieces under the bread guillotine fastened to the wall. Christabel had taken care to warn the children not to touch it; it was razor-sharp and dangerous in the wrong hands.

'But he doesn't write any more?'

Madame Normand gave her a shrewd look, shrugging. 'If he does, I never see him at it. Oh, all that is history! He is a farmer now, like his ancestors. When a man has land, it gets into his blood. The acting and writing, that was a young man's game, and he's no longer young. He'll be forty in two years. Life is a serious business when you reach that age. You start to realise that you're walking a downhill path, and you throw out all the games, the follies. I wouldn't be surprised if he got married again, got himself a son to inherit the *château*.'

'Oh, wouldn't you?' a sardonic voice said from the door, and Christabel started violently, looking round with big, confused amber eyes.

Madame Normand was not alarmed by his unheard arrival. 'Ah, you are up at last! Good morning!' she said, calmly placing the sliced bread in a straw basket and putting it in the middle of the table. She put the croissants next to it, and laid out cups and saucers. 'Your coffee is ready, strong and hot!'

'And I need it,' he said, sitting down and stretching an arm across the table to take a croissant. 'As I'm sure the little English girl has told you, I got drunk last night, and I've got a devil of a head this morning.'

'Yes, she has told me, and I can see why you drank. I've been racking my brains, trying to think of someone who could come in and look after the children, but I can't think of anyone. You could advertise in town.' Madame Normand poured him black coffee, and pushed it over to him. He picked up the cup and sipped, closing his eyes briefly.

'Ah, that's better. A cup of this inside me and I'll feel more human,' he murmured, opening his eyes again to smile at her. Christabel watched that smile with an odd sensation inside her. The last thing she had expected of Roland de Bellème was charm, but as he smiled at the old woman there was distinct charm in his lean olive face.

'Come, sit down, have your breakfast, *mademoiselle*,' Madame Normand told her, pouring another cup for her.

She took a seat opposite Roland; he was looking down into his coffee-cup, his face abstracted, and she risked a direct stare, following the hard bone-structure of temple, cheekbone, jaw. His mouth was taut, firmly moulded, passionate, his nose imperious. That was the final effect of his looks—an impression of power. His was a very male beauty: tough and insistent. His black hair showed no trace of grey; thickly vital, it sprang back from his forehead in a widow's peak, layered down the base of his neck, and cut short some way above the collar. He had the healthy tan of a man used to spending much time in the open air, and that made her wonder if Madame Normand was right—had he entirely given up the theatre? Was he too obsessed with his estates to care about writing plays?

She suddenly realised that while she was observing him, he in turn was watching her, dark eyes glittering through those lowered black lashes. She hurriedly looked away, turning pink.

'I must get down to town today, *madame*,' she said huskily. 'I have to check the times of the ferries to England from Brest, and book my passage on one. Is there a taxi service?'

'You're staying here!' Roland put down his cup and stared at her in challenge.

She shook her head obstinately, outfacing him. 'I'm sorry, but I really must go home. I'm sure you will find someone to take over—as Madame Normand just said, you can always advertise.'

'That will take time, and what am I to do meanwhile? No, you must stay for a few more days, give me time to get hold of someone else. Surely you can do that?'

Christabel had a sense of helpless frustration; she should never have permitted Eve-Marie to talk her into coming here in the first place. She should have insisted that Eve-Marie herself must deliver her children to Brittany. She had been weak-willed with Eve-Marie; she must not let Roland get away with manipulating her the way his sister-in-law had done!

'Just a few more days?' Roland murmured, watching her like a cat at a mousehole waiting for a mouse to venture out. He made her edgy; her teeth met as she crossly recognised the dilemma she faced.

Madame Normand very sensibly said, 'After all, my dear, that isn't too much to ask, is it? You can't leave two little girls here alone with Monsieur; he won't know how to cope with them, it wouldn't be fair to the children. Poor little mites! You wouldn't want them to go hungry, or not get put to bed because he had forgotten they were here, would you? But in two or three days Monsieur is bound to have found someone else!'

Christabel knew she was trapped. She stared across the table at Roland's crooked little smile; Roland knew she was trapped, too. His eyes mocked and held triumph because he had won this round, and there was nothing she could do about it except admit a temporary defeat.

# CHAPTER FOUR

'WHERE is your big dog?' Nina nervously asked her uncle as he dipped his flaky croissant in his coffee, and he bent sardonic dark eyes on her.

'He sleeps in a kennel outside. He isn't a house dog, he is a guard dog. That's why he is so fierce. Shall I bring him in to play with you?'

Nina shrank, shaking her head.

'No? Sure?'

'Don't tease her! She's afraid of him,' said Christabel, and he turned those glittering eyes on her, one brow rising.

'And you? What are you afraid of?'

She knew she was flushing, but with Madame Normand and the children watching she outfaced him, a defiant look in her eyes. Luckily, Dani provided a distraction by bursting out with the question she had been dying to ask for ages.

'Can we ride the horses?'

Roland slowly moved his gaze from Christabel to the child. 'Do you ride in Paris?'

Dani hesitated, reluctant to admit the truth, but Christabel said firmly, 'No, they have never ridden a horse, but I have, and I could teach them, if you have saddles.'

He leaned back in his chair, studying her, those heavy lids half drooping over ironic eyes. 'Are you an experienced rider?'

She had always lived in the country, and had been riding horses since she was small. She nodded and Roland abruptly got up.

'Show me.'

Startled, she stood up too, but gestured down at her candy-striped dress and bare legs. 'I'm not dressed to ride; I would have to change.'

He let his eyes wander over her, his mouth twisting. 'Yes—jeans would do. A pity, the sugar candy dress is very sweet, very young; it suits you.'

She flushed angrily. How old did he think she was? 'I've got some jeans and boots in my suitcase; I'll go and put them on!' She walked away and he called after her.

'We'll meet you at the field. I'll give the girls a lesson in saddling a horse while we wait for you.'

She heard Dani and Nina excitedly chattering to him as she made her way upstairs, and smiled. If he encouraged their obsession with the horses, he would soon win them over, and perhaps they would win him over, too, which would make it much easier for her when she had to go.

In her suitcase she found blue jeans and a T-shirt, a pair of boots, and a broad black leather belt. When she was dressed she considered her reflection, satisfied that he couldn't call her 'sweet' or 'young' any more. The clothes suited her better than anything else she possessed, and showed off her small waist and slender hips, the small, firm breasts. Ruefully, she admitted that there wasn't much they could do for her thin face, or her mousy hair, but you couldn't have everything!

When she reached the meadow, Roland had already saddled a fat old pony, and Nina was on its back, jogging along, her face blazing with de-light, while Roland led her around in a wide circle. Dani was sitting on the gate, drumming her heels against the bars, chewing a long piece of grass in her mouth, shouting advice to her sister.

She turned an excited face to Christabel. 'I had my turn first. I rode right round the field—well, nearly! It was great, Bel! I didn't bounce up and down, like Nina. I'm a natural rider—Roland said so. He said I had a natural seat on a horse, and I only fell off once, but I didn't hurt myself anyway, I fell in the grass.'

'Uncle Roland,' reminded Christabel. 'You must be careful, Dani! It's easy to have an accident when you start riding.'

'He said not to call him uncle. He said he hated being an uncle, it made him feel old, and we were to call him just Roland,' recited Dani smugly, with the triumph of being able safely to defy an adult.

Nina was waving; Christabel waved back, and climbed over the gate, very aware of Roland's narrowed stare. She walked towards the pony, her legs brushed by the meadow's long, seeding grasses, trying to ignore the way he watched her advance. Wild flowers blew among the grass: meadow but-tercup, musk mallow, flax, ox-eye daisy, scarlet poppy. She concentrated on enjoying their colour and gaiety to avoid Roland's dark eyes.

'I can see the horses haven't been in this field for long,' she said as she joined him and Nina.

He raised his brows. 'What makes you say that?'

'The grass is too long.'

He laughed. 'Observant. Yes, we turned them in here yesterday.'

'I told you I'd lived in the country most of my life.'

'So you did, but women don't always tell the truth.'

'You're too cynical,' Christabel said, bending to pick a buttercup which she wove into the pony's chestnut mane.

'Isn't she lovely?' Nina breathed, beaming. 'Her name is Clo-Clo. Her mother's name was Clothilde, so she was called Little Clothilde, but Roland shortened it to Clo-Clo.'

'You must call your uncle Uncle Roland,' scolded Christabel.

'I won't be called Uncle anything!' he said drily and she turned amber eyes up at him, frowning.

'I really think it's best that they call you uncle——'

'How old are you? Eighteen? Nineteen? Half my age, anyway...'

'Twenty,' she said quickly, and he pulled a face.

'As I said, half my age! Let me tell you here and now, *petite Anglaise*, I won't have you trying to force your opinions on me, or telling me how to treat a couple of little girls.' His voice was brusque, harsh, his face dark with irritation, and Dani and Nina looked anxiously at him, then at Christabel, who bit her lip.

'I'm sorry. Of course, it is up to you!'

'Yes,' he said, 'it is!' He slapped the pony's fat chestnut rump. 'Well, what do you think of Nina's riding?'

He seemed to find it easy to throw off his black moods, but Christabel was not so volatile. Huskily, she managed to say, 'It's very good; she looks as

if she has been riding for years.' To cover her confusion, she stroked the pony's broad nose and it
blew at her in a friendly way, snuffling at her shirt
to see if she had any food for it.

Roland suddenly lifted Nina down from the
pony's back and turned to Christabel. 'Let me see
how you ride!' Before she realised what he meant
to do, his hands closed on her waist and lifted her
up on to the pony as if she were a child little older
than Nina or Dani. The physical contact made her
tense, her face burning. Roland stepped back, re-
leasing her, and looked up, his head tilted.

'Well, show me what a good rider you are!' he
mocked, his dark eyes narrowed in observation of
her reaction.

It took her a moment to pull herself together,
then she gathered the reins into her hands, pressed
her trembling knees into Clo-Clo's fat sides, and
the pony casually ambled away. Christabel put her
into a jog and then into something of a canter,
although Clo-Clo was clearly not overjoyed by the
prospect of anything faster than a slow amble. She
moved a little faster for a while, then slowed to a
jog again as they returned towards the watching trio
by the gate. Christabel avoided Roland's watchful
gaze, her eyes fixed on the view of the *château*
behind him. It had a romantic aspect in the sunlight, like the Sleeping Beauty's castle set among
thorn trees. A wry smile crossed her face. Only in
this case it wasn't a princess who was locked away
in a frozen timelock, it was a prince—if you could
call Roland de Bellème a prince! He was hardly the
romantic type. He wouldn't thank her if he knew
what she was thinking; he would undoubtedly sneer.

She drew rein and swung down as she came level with him, but hurried to get back on the ground so that he should not have any excuse for grabbing her waist again.

He eyed her with dry understanding. 'Not show-jumping class, but you'll do,' he said, then murmured in a low tone, 'About last night...'

'I'd rather you didn't mention it!' Her face was hot and she couldn't meet his eyes.

He took no notice of her. 'I apologise for the way I behaved. If I hadn't been drunk, it would never have happened.'

How flattering, she thought, her head bent and her gaze fixed on the long grasses brushing her boots. He had to be drunk to want to make a pass at her, did he?

'It won't happen again,' he assured her. 'I hope you'll just forget the whole incident.'

'What incident?' she asked coolly, and he laughed.

'Thank you. That's very generous of you.'

She turned away from him to find Dani and Nina trying to take her place on the pony's back, pushing and shoving each other, squabbling like five-year-olds.

'My turn!' said Nina, red in the face.

'Isn't,' said Dani. 'My turn. Bel, isn't it? She had a ride last time; now it's my turn again, isn't it, Bel?'

'Yes, it's Dani's turn again,' decided Christabel, grateful for the interruption which gave her a chance to get over what Roland had said. She took time to show Dani how to mount, then gave her a brief lesson on the right way to sit, use her knees, and make the horse turn left or right.

All the time, though, she was thinking angrily about Roland. How did he expect her to forget what had happened last night? Did he think that sort of thing happened to her all the time? She might wish she could forget, she might pretend she had forgotten—but it was going to be a long time before she could put it out of her mind.

It wasn't the first time she'd been kissed; that wasn't it. She had been kissed by several young men, both at home in England, and since she had come to France. At the Sorbonne, the fact that she was English had made her different, intriguing, given her a certain cachet she had never had at home with local boys. She wasn't pretty enough to be a huge success, but she had dated several of the male students during the past two years. She hadn't slept with any of them. These days it wasn't fashionable to sleep around; people were far too conscious of the dangers of promiscuity. She hadn't even been tempted, because she hadn't yet fallen in love, and she couldn't bear the idea of going to bed with someone unless she loved him.

In any case, she wanted to get a good degree, and she had to stay in most evenings to babysit for Eve-Marie. Her free time was limited, her love-life merely casual. None of her dates had ever kissed her the way Roland had last night; he had had a drastic effect on her. She kept thinking about it, remembering the whirl of her senses, the heat and insistence of his kisses.

She wasn't a highly strung girl, but she had been frightened out of her wits for a time. He had been so strange, so violent; his eyes had had a strange glitter. The assault on her had come out of the blue—sometimes she almost believed she had dreamt the whole thing. She wished she had. But she would never be able to forget it, and she was angry with him for thinking that he only had to apologise for her to put the whole incident out of her mind.

She tried to stop thinking about it now, though. She had to concentrate on Dani and the pony, and forget Roland and what had happened last night— yet how could she when Roland was there, watching her? He made her intensely self-aware and nervous. Thank heavens he couldn't see inside her head, or guess what she was thinking. Although at times she almost felt he could!

'Well, I must go,' he suddenly said from the gate. 'I have more important things to do.'

Christabel threw a furious look at his back as he strolled away. He had more important things to do! So did she, back home in England, yet he calmly expected her to stay on here at his convenience, to look after his nieces while he got on with the 'more important things' he had to do!

'Don't forget to place that advertisement,' she shouted after him, her voice thick with fury.

He raised a casual hand without turning round, and she seethed—would he do it? She didn't know why she was letting him keep her here. He was utterly ruthless in getting his own way, and she did not trust him an inch.

His sister-in-law was no better, mind you! Eve-Marie shouldn't have sent her there, knowing Roland didn't want the children. But then, Eve-

Marie was pretty ruthless, too. How could any mother cheerfully dump her children without being sure they would be OK? She had gambled that Roland, faced with a *fait accompli*, would let them stay. She had gambled that Christabel wouldn't abandon them, either.

Christabel had always liked her, until now. At this moment, she did not like Eve-Marie at all, and when she came back to Paris in the autumn she would not be returning to Eve-Marie's apartment!

'Isn't it my turn again yet, Bel?' pleaded Nina, and Christabel dragged her attention back to the children, agreeing and telling Dani to climb down from the pony's broad back.

When she and the children returned to the *château* there was no sign of Roland. Madame Normand was polishing the panelling as they walked through the hall on their way to wash and change.

'You two look as if you've had a good morning!' she teased the little girls, and they giggled, bursting out with an account of their adventures.

Madame Normand exchanged smiles with Christabel over their heads, then said, 'Lunch is at one o'clock, *mes enfants*—so you had better hurry up and get washed and changed. You can't eat good food with dirty hands!'

'What is for lunch? We're starving!' Dani said, flushed from their hours in the open air, her hair windblown, her clothes grass-stained where she had fallen off the pony's back half a dozen times.

'It's a surprise,' said Madame Normand, collecting up her cleaning utensils and neatly piling them back into the large wicker basket in which she kept them. 'The first one down can help me in the kitchen, though.'

They raced off excitedly, each wanting the honour of helping her; she fascinated them because she was so unlike anyone they had ever known before, and while she was such a novelty in their lives they loved to be with her. Christabel saw them disappear into the bathroom, and went to lay out their clean clothes on their beds. That afternoon, she must find the washing machine. They were going through their clothes at an alarming rate.

When they were dressed, she let them rush back down to the kitchen, telling them that she would be along in ten minutes. She was aching from head to foot, too, it was so long since she had ridden, and her muscles were protesting violently. She ran a hot bath, flung in handfuls of scented bath crystals, slid gratefully into the water and lay there soaking her weary limbs for ten minutes until, with great reluctance, she made herself climb out. She must not keep Madame Normand's lunch waiting!

She wrapped a big white bath towel around herself, anchored it under her arms so that it covered her from her breasts down to her thighs, and walked out into the corridor, not expecting anyone else to be in that part of the house. A sound startled her. Looking round, she gave a gasp of shock, face burning, as she saw Roland just a few feet away, staring.

She shot across the corridor into her bedroom and slammed the door, leaning on it, breathing rapidly, her eyes shut, as if trying to expunge the memory of the way he had looked at her. Those dark eyes of his were so brilliant, so disturbing.

The towel had seemed no protection; she had felt naked under his hard gaze.

She must get away from here—and soon.

She dressed with shaky fingers in a green shift dress she had made herself last year, with Eve-Marie's help. She had little money for clothes, and bought second-hand things either from street markets or from fellow students. Eve-Marie didn't have much money either, but she was an excellent dressmaker. She said if she hadn't been able to get a stage role she had often taken a job as a seam-stress in a theatrical production, and she could make an attractive garment out of odds and ends of fabric. She had offered to teach Christabel to make her own clothes, but it had soon become ap-parent to both of them that Christabel had more thumbs than fingers. She had made a few simple items, and then ruefully given up trying.

When she got downstairs lunch was on the table: a big bowl of crisp home-grown salad with a French dressing poured over it; a selection of cold h'ors-d'oeuvres; a platter of cold sliced meats, cheese and fruit.

The children had helped lay the table and were already sitting at it, waiting impatiently for her. Roland was there, too, reading a newspaper, and Madame Normand was slicing more of the bread she had brought that morning.

'I'm sorry I'm late,' Christabel said, sliding into the empty chair.

Roland looked at his watch, frowning. 'It would be a help if you could be punctual for meals!' he snapped. 'Madame Normand has plenty of other things to do before she can go home.'

She turned to apologise again, to Madame Normand, who shrugged her thin shoulders and grimaced. 'It doesn't matter, *mademoiselle*.'

Christabel turned angry amber eyes on Roland, who silently offered her the salad bowl, his face hard. She took some salad, gave some to the children, handed the bowl back to Roland, who had meanwhile taken cold meat and cheese, and a slice of bread. He had some salad. Madame Normand poured white wine into his glass and offered the bottle to Christabel, who shook her head.

'I never drink at lunchtime or I go to sleep!' she said, and Madame Normand smiled amusement. Roland ignored the remark. He ate without lifting his head, or saying a word. Christabel was busy with the children, secretly glancing at him now and then, puzzled. Surely his grim look and silence were not entirely due to the fact that she had been ten minutes late for lunch?

He left before the rest of them had finished, saying curtly, 'I'm going into town to place that advertisement.'

'Good,' said Christabel and got another of his icy stares. He was a very moody man, she thought as he walked out of the room.

She offered to help Madame Normand clear the table and wash up, but the old woman said, 'Today, Dani and Nina have offered to help me, and afterwards we are going to make a special gateau for tea!'

'And it's a surprise for you, Bel, so you can't stay in the kitchen,' Dani said excitedly.

Nina danced up and down, beaming. 'We'll call you when it's ready.'

'You can go and study!' Dani told her with an adult intonation.

'Oh, thanks!' Christabel said, but she went upstairs to find the collection of Maupassant's short stories she was currently reading. It was both pleasure and work for her to read this particular book, so she curled up outside in the sunshine on the grass bank of the moat, watching the dark, cold water flow by.

After reading several of the short stories, though, she lay back on the warm grass and closed her eyes. Brittany had a mild, wet climate, rather windy on this Atlantic coast at times, but this afternoon it was quite hot in the summer sunshine, and she felt herself drifting off to sleep.

She woke up with a start when a seagull flew overhead and screeched. Sitting up, yawning, and flushed by the sun, Christabel looked at her watch, and was surprised to see that she had been asleep for an hour.

She picked up her book and went back into the chateau, knocked at the kitchen door and heard agitated cries from Dani and Nina.

'You can't come in! Go away! We aren't finished yet!'

She laughed and called to them, 'I'll go up to my room, then.'

It was as she was going through the hall that she remembered the telephone. Where could it be? And why had Roland denied he had one when she was absolutely certain Eve-Marie had told her she had rung him at the *château*? Had Eve-Marie lied? Well, she had lied about Roland agreeing to have the children, and Christabel wouldn't be surprised if she had lied about ringing him—yet somehow she believed Eve-Marie and doubted Roland's word.

There had been something in his face, a narrowing of his eyes, a look which wanted to deceive. He did not want her to use the telephone, but he had one—the question was where?

She had to ring her family soon. They would start getting worried about her. Feeling justified, she put her book down on a table and began searching the rooms on the ground floor, then went up to the first floor. She looked in all the bedrooms, even Roland's, noting how tidy it was now. Madame Normand must have done it that morning while they were all out with the horses.

She felt uneasy in the room and only stayed long enough to be certain that it did not hold a telephone. The bed held a strange fascination for her. She stood staring at it, remembering him lying there only that morning. It had been a shock to her to find out that he slept naked. Just remembering it made her blush to her hairline.

She backed out, averting her eyes from the bed. Well, there was no phone in that room! Hesitating in the corridor, she stared at a narrow, winding stone staircase which began in the corner of the wall by the leaded window. Where did that go? To the next floor, obviously. She looked out of the window, calculating that the stairs must lead up inside one of the conical towers.

She was nervous about going up there. After all, she had some excuse for being on the first floor, since her own bedroom was on it—but what possible reason could she give for prying about on the floor above this? What if Roland caught her? What on earth would she—could she—say?

She put a foot on the lowest stair, listened, and heard nothing but the gentle cooing of some wood pigeons among the trees, a sleepy summer sound which was usually comforting but which at that instant made her jump.

Roland might have a study up there—and that would be the obvious place to have a phone, wouldn't it?

She crept up the stairs and found herself outside a small, arched wooden door studded with iron nails. Christabel listened again, heard nothing at all this time, so she knocked on the door. Nobody answered. She grasped the round, iron doorknob and turned; the door slowly swung open and she stared into the room.

She wasn't sure what she had been expecting, but it hadn't been a book-lined study holding a desk, a leather swivel-chair, a music centre. Around the walls rose row upon row of books; she slowly ran a finger along the nearest row, moving into the room.

Did Roland work here? Was he secretly writing? Or did he just sit up here and read? She read the titles of some books. Novels. She turned and looked at the desk, and that was when at last she saw the telephone.

She went over to pick it up, heard the dialling tone and put it down again, biting her lip. Should she use it without Roland's permission? The cost of a call to England was bound to be quite high.

But he was keeping her here, against her will— she had every right to want to reassure her family!

She sat down in the leather chair and picked the phone up again, then put through the call to her home.

'Chris!' her mother said, sounding relieved. 'We had started to wonder what was happening! Where are you? Back in England?'

'No, I'm still in Brittany. I ran into a snag.' Could you call Roland de Bellème a snag? He was more of a giant obstacle.

'Is something wrong, darling?' Beverley Paget had a strong intuition, especially where her children were concerned. She was a small, sensitive, warm-hearted woman who painted water-colours and gardened in her leisure time, ran the home and still managed to work part time at the village school where she taught pottery. She always seemed to know when something was upsetting one of her children, and Christabel knew that she wouldn't be able to pull the wool over her mother's eyes; it had to be the truth—or most of it!

'Well...it seems that Eve-Marie didn't tell me everything,' she guardedly admitted, and told her mother what had happened.

'How naughty of her!' Mrs Paget said, and Christabel laughed.

'I said some stronger things about her when I realised what she had done! She was trying to railroad me into looking after her kids, although she knew damn well how I was looking forward to a few weeks at home.'

'Poor Chris,' her mother said sympathetically. 'So what is this famous playwright like? Is he interesting?'

Christabel was striken with dumbness by this casual question. Her mouth opened and shut as if she were a stranded fish, then she took a deep breath and said, 'He's selfish, rude, patronising, maddening, indifferent to other people's feelings, likes his own way all the time...'

'Darling!' her mother faintly said as she paused for another breath. 'Goodness! Well, I suppose being a writer he was bound to be a bit odd.'

Christabel couldn't help laughing at that, then groaning. 'Oh, Ma! Why are you always so keen to make excuses for people? Roland de Bellème is a monster, and the sooner I can get home, the better. He's advertising for someone to look after the children, so I could be able to come home in a few days' time. I'll keep in touch. Give my love to Dad.'

'What a pity he isn't here. You should have rung this evening, when he was back from school.' John Paget was the headmaster of the little village school where his wife taught pottery part time. He worked long hours and knew everyone in the village; he had taught many of them. The school was the centre of the village, and the Paget family had been totally involved in village life. The children were all grown-up now, and scattered, but John and Beverley Paget loved their home and were still absorbed in village life.

'Before you ring off, darling,' said her mother, 'Ginny says she and Dave are going to get married in the spring. Isn't that nice?'

'Lovely! Can I be a bridesmaid?' Her elder sister, Virginia, was an air stewardess, usually on the London to Rome run, and had been engaged to a flight engineer for a year without naming a date for the marriage.

'You can ask her when you get home. Darling, this call must be costing you a fortune!'

'Yes, I'd better ring off. See you soon. Love to everyone, especially Dad.'

Christabel replaced the phone and sat with closed eyes, the brief conversation having whirled her back to England, to her familiar home, the village, the family. That was where she belonged, that was real. This place was not real; it was magical, dreamlike, almost sinister at night. She didn't belong here, and she wished fervently that all of this were just a nightmare, and that when she opened her eyes she would wake up out of it.

Slowly she opened her eyes and she was still there, in the tower-room, Roland de Bellème's book-lined study. Sighing in disappointment, yet feeling a strange, tingling excitement, she leaned back in the chair and let her gaze wander around the room.

Close at hand on the bookshelves she saw, then, some bound copies of Roland's plays, both in French and in various translations. He had written four... no, five, she realised, leaning over to take down French copies of several, then an English translation of the most famous play. She sat there for a while, skimming over the pages with an interest she had always felt, but which was deepened now that she knew the writer personally. A play was different from a novel or a poem, in that it was harder to sense the personality of the writer. There was no narrator, no personality behind the characters—just the characters themselves speaking.

She was just as baffled and intrigued by the mind behind the plays, though. Roland was a strange man. She looked up again, frowning, to stare around the room as if hunting for answers to all the questions in her mind. There were paintings and little sculptures as well as books in the room. He seemed to like tiny stone carvings of birds and animals; they littered every free surface, and there were water-colours hanging on each side of the narrow windows.

The most striking was an oil-painting, though— it hung right opposite the desk, a large canvas framed in gold. The subject was the *château*; it dominated the twilight landscape in which it stood. She could see that night was falling from the sinking sun, the shadows it laid across the picture. There were figures in the foreground, too—gazing out at her, oddly posed in front of the drawbridge as if they had just left the *château*.

No doubt about the man—that was Roland, looking medieval, as he had on the night she and the children had arrived, only he wasn't wearing a cloaklike cape this time, just a black sweater and trousers. There was a woman with him, yet standing slightly apart, wearing filmy white, a long dress that also looked medieval, with long sleeves, a high neck, and full skirts that seemed to be blowing in the wind. A shadow seemed to fall between the two human figures; black and elongated, it stretched from out of view. Was it the shadow of a tree? Or a man?

Or... Christabel drew a shaken breath. Or was it the shadow of death?

She got up and went over to stare closer, trying to make certain what it was, but the closer you went the less you saw it. She backed again, watching the lovely face of the woman. It had to be Roland's wife, and she had been very beautiful. Long golden-red hair, green eyes, an oval face of milky delicacy— and an expression on that face which Christabel couldn't quite define. What did that look say?

'What the hell do you think you're doing?'

She swung round, trembling, as she met Roland's black and angry stare. He took a stride towards her, and Christabel was terrified by what she saw in his face.

# CHAPTER FIVE

Guilt made her stammer. 'I'm sorry, I was just——'

'Just what?' he snarled, reaching the desk and snatching up a copy of one of his plays, holding it up for her to see, throwing it down again with a crash that made her jump. 'Prying?'

'No! I only came up here to look for a telephone. I knew you had one, even though you lied to me.' She threw an accusation back at him, her chin lifted in defiance. 'It had to be somewhere, and I'd been through all the rooms downstairs.'

'Oh, had you?' His voice held a harsh note, his black brows were drawn. 'While I was out of the way you've been searching my house, have you?'

'Not searching it ... I was just looking——' She broke off, biting her lip. He was right, she had been prying through his house, reading his books, staring at the painting of him and his dead wife, the little sculptures ... these very private possessions, things he clearly did not want people to see, since he kept them in here, in his personal sanctum, hidden away.

She felt ashamed now, but she wouldn't admit it—not to him, not when he looked at her like that, with contempt and distaste. She felt impelled to defend herself, and she could only do that by attacking him, so that was what she did, her voice rising fiercely. 'You won't let me go home, as I had arranged, and you lied to me when I asked if I could

telephone my family—you lied! You said you had
no phone, but I knew you must have, because Eve-
Marie talked to you on the phone, and you more
or less admitted as much, yet you wouldn't let me
talk to my parents, and I was afraid they would be
worrying about me. I had to ring them soon.'

He stared at the phone. 'And you did?'

'Yes. I told them I was here, and that I'd be home
soon.'

'You'll be home when I manage to get someone
to look after the children and not before!' he said,
picking up all the copies of his plays and pushing
them back on to the shelves. 'And in future, you'll
keep out of my study, do you hear? This room is
off limits to everyone but myself, and that includes
Madame Normand. Do you understand? Never
come in here again!'

'I won't,' she said huskily, making for the door,
only to find him moving faster, getting between her
and her goal. She came to a halt, warily watching
him.

He was silent for a moment, his face taut, a little
tic flicking just below one eye. Suddenly he said,
'I saw you staring at the oil. I want your promise
to forget you ever saw it.'

Bewildered, she just stared, and his mouth
twisted.

'I don't want its existence known about, so I must
have your word that you won't tell a single soul
you've seen it.'

'Why?' she asked, baffled, and he frowned
angrily.

'Why? Why do you ask so many questions? Why
should I tell you, when if you hadn't come up here

to pry and poke about you wouldn't have seen it? I have every right to demand that you never tell anyone—' He broke off, staring down into her wide, bemused amber eyes. 'Oh, hell! Why shouldn't I tell you? What will any of it mean to you, anyway, you little schoolgirl? I wish I had a face like yours; a piece of nice blank paper for life to write on. You stare at me with those innocent, puzzled eyes and make me feel very old!'

'I'm sorry,' she said, chagrin in her face.

'Now you look insulted!'

'Wasn't that what you intended? To insult me?'

'Strangely enough, no,' he said with wry amusement. 'I meant what I said...I envy you. That's one of the ironies of life, you know—that the young always envy the middle-aged their experience of life, and the middle-aged always envy the young their happy state of innocence.'

'You're not middle-aged!'

'I'm nearly twice your age, as we've already established.' He put a hand out and stroked her cheek slowly. 'Skin like a baby's, not a line on it.' His index finger touched her mouth, slid along the trembling curve of it, making her intensely aware of his touch. 'And a mouth that's positively sinful,' he murmured, staring at it.

Christabel couldn't take her eyes off him, hypnotised by the deep, husky sound of his voice, by the seductive slide of his fingers. He still looked angry, yet she felt it was not with her.

'But women can be very deceptive,' he said harshly, his hand dropping from her. 'It never occurred to me that while I was out you would search the place, or I would have locked the painting away where you couldn't find it. But, since you did see it, I want your promise not to tell anyone. It's the work of a very famous artist. It was painted after...after my wife's death, and I bought it privately...' He frowned, staring down at her startled wide-set eyes. 'Secretly!' he stressed, as if she had forced the word out of him. 'Nobody knows I have it, and I don't want anyone to know. So, do I have your word of honour that you won't ever tell a living soul you saw it here?'

She was about to promise when a horrifying idea hit her, and she gave him a worried look. 'You aren't going to destroy it, are you? I know some people hate portraits of themselves or someone they love so much that they feel they have to get rid of them, destroy them, but this is such a good painting, it's an amazing likeness.'

He laughed with that terrible black anger, his gaze lifting from her face to flash across the room to where the painting hung. Watching him, Christabel saw contempt and bitterness twist his mouth, make his eyes burn like hot coal.

'Of her? Yes, amazing. It was done from memory, he hadn't forgotten anything. That's just how she looked.'

'I meant...you, it's a good likeness of you,' she whispered, appalled by the look on his face. His eyes flicked back to her. 'I don't know what your wife looked like, do I? I never knew your wife,' she said, then could have kicked herself for her insensitivity. It was obvious he still mourned for his wife. Even seven years after her death the emotion inside him was so powerful that Christabel felt herself trembling convulsively at the force of it.

'Well, take a good look,' he said roughly, taking her by the shoulders and turning her to face the canvas. 'Beautiful, wasn't she? Look at that hair, those eyes, that lovely body...'

Christabel looked, reluctantly, wishing she had never come into this room or seen that woman's golden beauty. She knew she would never forget it, or this moment, or the look on Roland de Bellême's dark face as he held her, his fingers cruel.

He swivelled her round to face him, bending towards her. 'Now tell me the truth! You're here to spy on me, aren't you?'

The accusation left her breathless, her mouth open, her eyes wide. 'Don't be ridiculous! Who would want... why should anyone want to spy on you?' Was he out of his mind? Why on earth should he imagine that people wanted to spy on him?

He grimaced, watching her closely. 'How much do you know, I wonder?'

'About what?' She watched him in turn, her amber eyes disturbed. Had loneliness and grief unhinged him? That wouldn't be so surprising, living alone here all this time, brooding over the death of his wife.

'What has Eve-Marie told you? Women always talk to each other, they're inveterate gossips. Eve-Marie wouldn't have sent you here without telling you—' He broke off, his eyes probing her upturned face. 'You know who painted that?' His head jerked sideways towards the oil-painting.

'No, I'm afraid...' She studied it briefly, shaking her head. 'I don't know much about contemporary French art. I don't recognise the style, but he's obviously very good. I mean, it's wonderful painting.'

He said a famous French name and her eyes widened in shock.

'Good heavens...no wonder you don't want anyone to know you've got it. It must be worth a fortune. You ought to have burglar alarms to protect it. I hope you've got it insured.'

He began to laugh harshly. 'What a sensible, down-to-earth little girl you are! No, it isn't insured, and yes, it is probably worth a fortune.'

Suddenly they both heard the children calling, far below—high, excited, happy voices which broke in on the tense atmosphere in the tower-room and made Christabel blink as if she had been a long way away for a very long time.

'Dani and Nina,' she said, as if he might not realise who it was calling her.

His mouth twisted. 'Yes. You'd better go down to them.' But he still held her shoulders and did not make any move to release her, his dark eyes brooding on her face. 'Eve-Marie's clever,' he said. 'Sending a little innocent like you was shrewd, but you can tell her it isn't going to work.'

He let go of her and she ran, out of the door, down the stairs, relieved to escape from that room, from Roland de Bellème and his books, his works of art, his memories. She wished she could get in touch with Eve-Marie and warn her that her famous brother-in-law was...what? Odd? Sick? Crazy?

Or did Eve-Marie know that? Had she sent them down here in the full knowledge that Roland was suffering delusions about being spied on? Would a mother send her children to stay with a crazy person? Christabel paused, frowning—but then what sort of mother sent her children to stay with someone who had refused point-blank to have them? Eve-Marie was obsessed with her career, ready to sacrifice anything to it, and no doubt she had been certain that she could trust Christabel to stay with Dani and Nina, in spite of her reluctance.

Roland was right—Eve-Marie was shrewd, a clever woman who understood other people. She had probably persuaded herself that the end justified the means. It was so easy to fool yourself.

Christabel grimaced. Look at the way I convinced myself I had every right to search this place to find a phone! she thought. I wish to God I hadn't. I'd give anything not to have seen that portrait, realised how beautiful his wife had been, seen the deep black grief he still feels for her...

'Bel! Where are you? Bel?' called the children, and she shook herself out of her mood and put on a light, false voice to answer them.

They had made her a large strawberry gâteau—several layers of sponge cake filled with whipped fresh cream and sliced strawberries. Faces shining with pride, they watched her as she admired it.

'Amazing! Am I going to get a slice now? I love strawberries!' she said, and they looked self-important.

'Not yet! It isn't time!'

'You must wait for English teatime,' said Madame Normand, smiling. 'The children want English sandwiches, with cucumber, and a pot of tea, and then...'

'The gâteau!' the two little girls chorused, and Madame nodded.

'And then the gâteau!'

Christabel made the sandwiches and the tea, and they all sat down around the kitchen table to enjoy an English tea together.

'Shall we send some up to Monsieur de Bellème?' asked Christabel, but Madame Normand shook her head.

'He will expect his dinner at the usual time. I go home for a few hours, and come back to serve dinner and clear away for him.'

Having now discovered how far she had to cycle to her home and back to the *château*, Christabel looked horrified. 'While I'm here, why not let me serve dinner and clear away? I'm quite happy to do it, *madame*, especially as you've taken the children off my hands this afternoon. I really appreciated that, it was very kind of you. Let me repay it by serving the dinner for you.'

Madame Normand hesitated, but allowed herself to be persuaded, since the meal was quite a simple one and only needed to be served. She left an hour later, telling Christabel that there was a rabbit and prune terrine in the fridge, a *coq au vin* in the oven.

'No need to cook a vegetable—the potatoes are in the pot with the mushrooms and chicken now. I just added them. Monsieur likes his dinner served around seven, he keeps early hours. And if Monsieur is still hungry, I've made one of my strawberry tarts. He likes them better than anything else, and we have to use up the strawberries from the garden. I got the children to pick me a basket of them, and they overdid it!'

Christabel laughed. 'And ate a few on the way, I've no doubt!'

'Oh, no doubt! But they were good children this afternoon. That Dani will make a cook one of these fine days. Ah, it is good to have children in the house. A pity Monsieur doesn't marry again and get himself a family. Just because one woman is no good, it doesn't mean they are all the same.'

Christabel stiffened, eyes widening, but before she could ask Madame Normand what she meant the housekeeper was bustling out of the door, and the children were still within earshot, anyway.

Turning, her face uncertain, Madame Normand asked, 'Sure you can manage dinner without help?' and Christabel nodded smiling.

Christabel sent the little girls to play in their bedroom at half-past six, telling them to be in bed by eight-thirty and went downstairs to check that everything was ready for dinner at seven. Madame had laid the table in the kitchen, which was where Roland ate all his meals unless he had company.

Christabel cut slim wedges of terrine and put them on plates decorated with salad: butterflies of thinly sliced cucumber, tomato flowers, an edging of mixed French lettuce which she also found in the fridge: frisée and oak-leaf and lamb's-lettuce.

She lit the candle in the centre of the table, stood back to admire the effect, and then, before calling Roland de Bellème, she checked on the chicken in the oven. The smell of it was mouth-watering, a fork test told her it was meltingly cooked, so she turned off the oven and went to the foot of the stairs.

She didn't need to call Roland, he was already coming down. The grandfather clock chimed seven as his feet touched the bottom stair, and

Christabel's mouth quirked sideways. He was either hungry, or expected his meal to be on the table precisely at the same time each evening!

He eyed her in a frowning silence, from head to foot. She lifted her chin in self-defence. If he didn't approve of her only other good dress, too bad! She had very few decent clothes. In Paris, she largely wore jeans and shirts or sweaters: student uniform. It helped you not to stand out, to be accepted. She knew it also suited her looks.

'Where's Jeanne—Madame Normand?' he grimly demanded, and she explained.

'She left you to make the dinner?' He sounded furious.

'She cooked it, I'm just serving it.' With a trace of resentful sarcasm, she said, 'That isn't beyond me!' She swung on her heel and walked back into the kitchen, aware of him following, staring at her rear.

She wished she hadn't put this black dress on. It had originally been bought from a fellow student who had worn it for a family funeral. It was utterly plain and unadorned, and she didn't like wearing black, but she couldn't wear the green one all the time. Who knew how long she was going to be stuck here? A pity this dress was rather too tight—she had had it for over a year now, and had obviously put on some weight since her first year at university. It clung all the way down, over her breasts, her hips, her buttocks, which made her very self-conscious with Roland's eyes fixed on her.

'I couldn't find any wine,' she said over her shoulder. Madame Normand had laid the table with fine crystal glasses, so she obviously intended wine to be served, but she hadn't chilled any in the fridge.

'What's for dinner?' Roland abruptly asked. She told him and he nodded.

'I'll get wine from the cellar; you'd better come and see where to look, and next time you can get it yourself.' He led the way across the kitchen into another corridor which she had not yet explored. Opening a door, Roland took down a storm lantern hanging on the wall inside. He lit the wick and turned up the light, then led the way down steep wooden steps into a cave-like cellar. Christabel followed close behind him, her hand nervously gripping a rail fixed into the wall.

The cellar was enormous, with a low beamed roof and clammy stone walls. The swinging circle of light from Roland's lantern gave glimpses of it, filled with wooden shelving holding row upon row of dusty bottles of wine, thick cobwebs woven between them. The sound of footsteps echoed in the cavernous interior, startling her, but Roland didn't seem to notice; he walked unhesitatingly to one part of the cellar. Christabel stayed at the foot of the stairs at first, looking around, listening to the eerie echoes. Then, suddenly realising that she couldn't see or hear Roland any more, she gave a little gasp of alarm and ran towards the gap he had taken, between rows of wine-bins, expecting to see the light from his lantern as soon as she reached the end of the row.

Instead, she faced blackness and silence. Her eyes probed and searched in vain, so she ran on to the next little opening. Again, no sign of Roland; no sound, either.

'Roland!' she called shakily, then heard a movement right behind her. She spun, saw nothing for a second, then heard the sound again, a strange pattering noise on the stony, sanded floor of the cellar. Christabel looked down and saw the gleam of eyes in the darkness.

She gave a yell of fear and revulsion. 'A rat!' She turned wildly to dash back towards the cellar stairs, and ran full tilt into a firm male body.

She screamed again, louder, as an arm went round her.

'Stop that noise!' Roland's deep voice ordered, and her head fell back as she looked up in relief. 'Oh, it's you!'

'Who in God's name did you think it was?' His sardonic tone made her angry.

'I saw a rat!' she burst out hoarsely. 'It was enormous! I heard a scraping noise and looked down and saw its eyes, as close to me as you are now—over there, in the dark . . .' She pointed, then looked up at him accusingly. 'You left me in the dark and a rat came right up to me. I almost stepped on it . . .' A shudder of atavistic fear ran through her at the very idea. 'You ought to have electric light down here, and you shouldn't have left me!'

'I told you to come with me! You shouldn't have got left behind.' He held the lantern down at his side, the light making a circle around their feet, but leaving their faces in darkness. Under that arm he had a dusty bottle of wine; his other arm was around Christabel. His eyes glittered down at her, like the eyes of the rat: strange, menacing, hypnotic.

It was only at that instant that she realised how she was clinging to him, her hands gripping his shoulders, her body pressing close, her breasts against his chest, her hips and thighs suddenly aware of the warmth and closeness of his.

She stiffened and let go of him, tried to back away, but came up against the encircling arm keeping her there.

'I'm sorry you were frightened,' he said softly, and the arm tightened, pulling her closer again.

'We'd better go back...the dinner...I have to...' She was stammering, her throat tight and hot, her body trembling, and Roland's face was inexorably moving down towards her.

'Shh...' he whispered as his mouth closed over hers, but he didn't have to urge silence because the first hot touch of his mouth made her dumb, her whole system shocked into temporary paralysis by the sensual impact of his kiss. She couldn't move, couldn't speak, couldn't think. She didn't even know what was happening to her.

Roland broke off the kiss abruptly, almost pushing her away, his arm withdrawn, his body suddenly a foot away as he stared down at her through the darkness.

'You asked for that, I'm not apologising this time,' he muttered in a harsh voice. 'You threw yourself at me, and I'm not superhuman.' He turned on his heel and began to go back up to the kitchen, the circle of light from the lantern swinging around him.

Violently shaking, Christabel couldn't follow him for a moment. Only now that it was over did she surface from her sensuous trance. Her lips burnt from the fierceness of that kiss, her body ached and yearned. She felt boneless, her eyes blind with the passion that had flared between them. Roland had not been gentle. In the demand of his mouth she had learnt a great deal about him, had felt the pressure of need, frustration, desire, and with all that another emotion, an angry resentment of the other three, a reluctance to admit any emotion at all.

She had difficulty standing, let alone moving. Her face was feverish, her hands icy and trembling; shame was eating her up. He was right, she had thrown herself into his arms, clung, pressing herself against his body. She couldn't deny it, nor could she deny the sensual hunger she felt, but she was angry with him—with herself, too.

She hadn't intended to fling herself at him; she hadn't knowingly wanted him to kiss her, but she could never risk telling Roland that. Not merely because he wouldn't believe her, but because to convince him that any invitation to him had come from her unconscious mind would betray her just as much.

Roland's reactions to her were just as complex as hers to him. He didn't want to want her; she had felt his anger as strongly as she felt her own now. It made Roland furious to need a woman, to feel the intolerable urge of his own sexuality.

Roland still loved his dead wife, and to desire a living woman was to betray the dead one.

'What are you doing now?' his harsh voice grated from the top of the cellar steps, the lantern light flashing downwards to pick her out from the darkness.

She looked down, to hide her face from that searching light, and began shakily to climb the steps.

Roland let her pass him, her eyes lowered. He shut off the lantern light, then rehung the lantern on the wall in the cellar while Christabel hurried back to the kitchen. When he joined her Roland uncorked the wine and poured it, then washed his hands before sitting down to eat dinner.

It was not until they were eating the *coq au vin* that he spoke again. 'Jeanne makes this superbly! What do you think? Good, isn't it? This is one of my birds. I killed it for her two days ago. She likes to tenderise them well before cooking them.'

It was a shock to her how calm and normal his voice sounded. He had himself under control once more. Christabel was afraid to trust her own voice. It might shake. She wished she could extinguish the fever he had lit in her as easily as he had shut off the lantern light.

She had put some food into her mouth as he spoke, to give herself an excuse for not answering at once. Swallowing reluctantly, she finally murmured, 'It's delicious.'

'More wine?' He refilled her glass and she took it gratefully, taking a mouthful. 'You like it? It comes from a friend's vineyard. She has a small place on the Loire, turns out good stuff one year in ten. This is one of the good years. She sends me a case for my birthday every year.'

'Lucky you.' The wine was making it easier to talk. Christabel drank some more and felt it warm her throat. 'It tastes of sun and apples,' she said, closing her eyes to drink.

He laughed, surprising her. 'It tastes of grapes,' he said with dry derision. 'What could be better than that? And what would you know of wine, anyway, a little English schoolgirl like you?'

She opened amber eyes and glared at him. 'In Paris we drink wine every day with our dinner! I've learnt a lot since I came to France.'

'I know the students at the Sorbonne. Oh, they drink wine, but cheap muck from the supermarkets—vinegar masquerading as wine!' He lifted his glass, peered through the ruby glow of it. 'Now this is the real thing! You can taste the sunshine in it. And stop swallowing it at that speed—you'll get drunk and never taste the wine at all. Take a mouthful, roll it round your tongue, let the flavour of it coat your whole mouth...'

Christabel obeyed, half closing her eyes to experience the taste better. 'Mmm...lovely,' she said, her voice drowsy, and Roland laughed. She opened her eyes again and he grimaced at her over the table.

'Do you want to be an actress, by any chance?'

Startled, eyes wide, she shook her head. 'An actress? No—why?'

He stopped smiling, his dark eyes sardonic. 'I'm still trying to work out why my sister-in-law was so determined to get you over the drawbridge and strand you here!'

Christabel frowned, lowering her glass to the table. 'But...why should you think I might be an actress?'

'Because sometimes people try to get me to write plays for a particular actor or actress.' He considered her, mouth twisting. 'Although it's usually someone famous, not a little nobody.'

She gave him a resentful look. 'Thanks. You seem to take a lot of pleasure in insulting me—I don't know why... What have I ever done to you?'

'You've invaded my life! And I can't get rid of you until I find someone else to take care of those brats—isn't that injury enough without making yourself a walking, breathing temptation?' The anger breathed in his voice, like fire on a bush wind, and she tensed in alarm, shooting to her feet to clear the plates from the table.

'There's strawberry tart, if you want a dessert,' she muttered as she stacked the dirty china on the draining-board.

'No, I've had enough to eat, thanks.' He emptied the last of the wine into his own glass, pushing back his chair.

'Coffee?'

'Bring it into the drawing-room,' he said, vanishing, and she looked after him with a grimace of resentment. He was leaving her with all the washing-up and expecting her to wait on him, too, bringing his coffee to him in the drawing-room! Well, she wasn't sitting in there with him. She would take her own coffee here in the kitchen after she had put everything in the dishwasher.

When she carried the coffee-tray into the drawing-room he was lying back in an armchair, reading a book, his empty wine-glass balanced on the arm of the chair.

He looked up as she placed the tray on a low table and then carried that over to the side of his chair. 'Oh, thanks.' He gave a swift glance at the single cup on the tray. 'You aren't having any?'

'No,' she said. 'I'm going to bed now. Goodnight, *monsieur*.'

'Bed this early?' He shot a look at his watch. 'It's barely nine o'clock!'

'I have to get up early with the children.' She stood there demurely, hands clasped in front of her waist, eyes lowered. Through her lashes she was absorbing the fact that he was reading poetry; she couldn't read the name of the poet, and wondered whose work he liked.

There was a little silence; she risked an upward glance to meet his eyes. 'What did you say you were studying at the Sorbonne?' he asked, and she told him again. He held out his book to her. 'Do you know his work?'

She read the poet's name and exclaimed. 'Oh, yes! I discovered him this year. He's very good, one of the best modern French poets, I think. So simple, but every word counts.'

'Which is your favourite?' he asked, and she began to turn the pages, hunting for one poem.

'Sit down a moment,' Roland said, and she perched on the edge of a chair nearby while she found the right page.

'This is probably my favourite!' She held out the book to him, but he shook his head.

'Read it to me.'

Christabel went a little pink. 'Oh, well... I think you'd better read it yourself, I'm not very good at reading aloud!'

'Read it, don't be so damn coy!'

She clenched her teeth at the abrupt tone and words, then swallowed, her head bent. 'Oh, very well, but don't say I didn't warn you.'

She read the poem huskily. It wasn't very long, and the words were like drops of clear, pure water, instantly understandable, intensely telling.

When she ended, Roland sighed. 'Yes. I know it, of course. You're right, it is one of his best.'

A silence fell between them. After the poem there seemed nothing else to say. She dropped the book on to the table, next to his tray of coffee. 'Well, goodnight,' she said, and this time he did not try to detain her.

## CHAPTER SIX

THE following day Christabel didn't set eyes on Roland until the evening. By the time she and the children came down from breakfast, he was working in the fields, Madame Normand told them, placing *petits pains au chocolat*, little pastry rolls filled with dark, sweet chocolate, in front of the children. She had coffee for Christabel, and croissants.

'And what are you going to do today?' she asked quizzically, eying Dani and Nina in their jeans and T-shirts. 'Let me guess!'

'Ride the horses!' they said, and Madame Normand said it with them, her brown face indulgent.

'The horses, the horses! What else? Why did I ask?'

'Don't eat so fast,' Christabel scolded as they pushed their pastries into their mouths. 'And drink some of your delicious hot chocolate!'

They had finished long before she had drunk her coffee, and fidgeted on their chairs, kicking their legs back and forth, watching her with suffering expressions as she ate.

'Can't we go and watch the horses until you come?'

'You'll go into the field, and that could be dangerous.'

'We won't! Promise, word of honour!' Dani turned beseeching eyes on her. 'Oh, please, Bel! We're wasting time.'

'All right. You can run on ahead, but do *not* go into the field, or anywhere near the horses, until I arrive. Just stay outside the gate and watch them. Don't even pat them or give them that apple I saw you hide in your pocket, Nina!'

Nina pulled a face. 'Oh, but I can give it to Clo-Clo when you come?'

'Yes, but not before!'

'Promise, promise,' they said, running like the wind.

Madame Normand laughed as the door banged behind them. 'Oh, it must be so good to be that age, and with such exciting things happening all the time!'

'Yes,' sighed Christabel, envying them that eager rushing, the utter lack of secrecy over what they wanted. Dani and Nina didn't even think to hide how they felt. It must be such a relief to let emotion pour out without fearing ridicule or embarrassment.

Madame Normand eyed her with amusement, shaking her head. 'Oh, but you're young yourself! The milk scarcely dry on your nose! You've got a whole life in front of you. I was talking about older people—like myself, or Monsieur de Bellème. Our lives are slower, full of customary happenings; we know what to expect of each day, each month, each year. Life has no more surprises, at my age, and that's just as it should be. I may envy the little girls, but it would make my head spin to be running about all day waiting for new and exciting things to jump out at me!'

Christabel finished her coffee and stared down into the empty cup, frowning. 'Monsieur isn't so very old,' she said in a low voice.

Madame Normand was clearing away the children's plates and bowls of half-drunk chocolate. 'Well, no, that's true, but when that wife of his was killed he gave up living, too. Myself, I can't understand it, letting a bitch like that ruin his life, even after she is dead, but who can fathom a man's mind? There are women like that who can ruin a man forever, you know. It's an obsession, like the children have for the horses. She had that effect. Not just on Monsieur Roland. Others, too, were obsessed with her. An artist who came here all the time, painting her, watching her, mooning after her like a crazy man—and poor Monsieur Hilaire——' She broke off, clicking her tongue angrily. 'Oh!' She spat out a word that made Christabel jump and flush. 'I shouldn't talk, that's it! I should put a padlock on my teeth. Forget I said it, *mademoiselle*. I've no business talking about the family, and he'd be very angry with me if he knew.'

'I won't tell him,' Christabel said, getting up, although she was eaten with curiosity. Had Eve-Marie's husband fallen in love with his brother's wife? Surely that wasn't what Madame Normand meant? 'I must catch up with the children,' she said, hurrying out, longing to stay and ask questions, yet realising she couldn't do it.

Madame Normand was genuinely angry with herself; she hadn't been pretending dismay just now as she had caught back whatever she had been about to say. Christabel guessed that she sometimes talked freely about the Bellèmes to her own family, or to

local people who had known them for years, and
already knew the scandals and secrets of the
*château*'s owners, but Christabel was an outsider,
and, even worse, English! Madame Normand
couldn't be sure she would not repeat whatever she
heard.

Throughout that long, sunny day Christabel tried
to stop herself thinking about Roland and the hints
Madame Normand had dropped that morning. It
wasn't her business; she ought to forget all about
it, which was what Madame Normand would wish,
not to mention Roland himself. His wife had been
dead for seven years, and Eve-Marie's husband was
dead, too. Whatever had happened was buried in
the past, and should stay that way.

That was what she kept telling herself—but it
wasn't easy to block out the questions which kept
popping into her head, questions which had begun
to trouble her when she had seen Eve-Marie in
Roland's play, had been bowled over by its strange
power and then discovered that the playwright had
stopped writing and become a recluse.

The mystery of Roland de Bellème's disap-
pearance from the Paris theatre scene had intrigued
her long before she had actually met him; now that
she knew him she would love to know why he had
abandoned Paris and the theatre world for this
eerie, isolated spot.

There were parts of Brittany to which tourists
flocked in droves, little seaside resorts with new
bungalow developments above the long sandy
beaches, promenades packed with restaurants and
cafés, all the usual clutter of modern
holidaymaking.

Roland's *château* stood in a very different part of the region. The nearby town was from another century, a faded remnant of the Edwardian seaside holiday. Winds blowing in from the Bay of Biscay battered the dunes of sand along the coast, attacked the grey slate roofs and solid walls of old houses, uprooting great trees and leaving glistening white salt spray over everything in their path. There were few houses outside the town, few cars on the roads. The landscape was bleak and empty, as haunted and mysterious as Roland's last play.

Was that why he had come back here? Did he feel that this was where he belonged? He had grown up here, his family had lived here for generations— this place must be part of his blood and bones.

That might explain why he had come back here to live permanently—but why had he also stopped writing? And how did his brother's death fit into the pattern? Not to mention the death of his wife! Why didn't he want anyone to know that he had that painting of himself and his wife? She simply did not believe he was afraid of being burgled!

There were many questions, and no certain answers. Her thoughts went round and round inside her head like a mouse in a cage looking for a way out.

Dinner that evening was just as beautifully cooked, fish soup followed by veal and then raspberry tart. Roland appeared exactly on time as he had the previous evening, but Christabel had wine on the table this time, though, so that there was no risk of another trip with him down into the cellar. She had gone down to get it herself with the aid of an electric torch.

She had just placed the steaming tureen on the table when she heard his footsteps. 'Good evening,' she said without turning round, and ladled soup into the deep soup-plates.

'Good evening.' Roland leaned past her to pick up the bottle of wine; his shoulder touched her and she jerked slightly, as if the little contact had sent a flash of electricity through her. Soup splashed over on to the tablecloth; a thin reddish stain spread through the white linen, and she bit her lip, setting down the bowl.

'Now what made you do that?' Roland drawled, his tone sardonic.

She ran to get a damp cloth in the hope of getting the worst of the stain out before it spread, and he watched her efforts with his black brows lifted in amusement. She kept her eyes down, avoiding his stare, deeply self-conscious.

'Did you choose this?' Roland asked, putting the bottle of wine back on the table.

'Yes. Isn't it OK?' She finished ladling out soup as he sat down.

'Veal today, isn't it? Yes, it's fine, and you've chilled it perfectly. A white Burgundy should be this temperature—not too cold or it loses taste.' He filled her glass. 'Taste it before you eat—or do you know it?'

She shook her head, sitting down, wishing he would not watch her as she picked up her glass and took a mouthful, then rolled it around as he had shown her the previous night to let the full flavour of the wine reach her palate.

'It's very good,' she said shyly when she had swallowed.

'You picked well, even though you didn't know what you were doing. You have the right instincts, all you need is someone to give you a few lessons. While you're here I might educate you a little.'

There was a disturbing mockery in his eyes and Christabel wasn't quite sure what he meant by educating her a little. She looked down at her soup and hurriedly said, 'We mustn't let this get cold!'

He laughed softly and helped himself to the *roux*, a hot, mustardy paste which had to be stirred into the soup, then he sprinkled on to it some of the grated cheese and croutons which Jeanne Normand had placed on the table. Christabel took some, too, rather gingerly. She had watched Madame Normand make the fish soup that afternoon, using cheap fish which she said she had bought down at the quayside in the town early that morning. Christabel wasn't sure she was going to like the result, especially with the powerful *roux* stirred into it, but in fact the soup was delicious.

'Why didn't you study English literature, in England?' Roland asked her as they were eating the next course, a complete contrast: thin slices of pan-fried, breadcrumbed veal plainly served with wedges of lemon, boiled potatoes and green beans. 'Why French literature and in France?'

'I wanted to live in France, become fluent in the language... I was very attracted to France, I suppose.'

'And your family? What do they think?'

'My parents were happy about it.'

'What did you say your father did for a living?'

'He's the headmaster of the school.'

'In his village?'

She nodded. 'Little Wascombe.'

'Little what?' She repeated it and he laughed, black eyes dancing. 'How strange you English are with your place names . . . Little Wascombe! And so your father is a big man in this village? The local headmaster; everyone knows him, he is important to them all?'

'I suppose you could say that. He's very involved in village life, anyway, and so is my mother.'

'She teaches too?'

'Pottery, part time, and adult evening classes in pottery, too. My mother is always busy with something.'

'You're like her?'

'To look at? No, I wish I were.' Christabel removed the plates and placed the raspberry tart on the table. 'Do you want some of this?'

'Certainly, it's one of my favourites.' He refilled his glass and made a face. 'That's the end of the wine. Too bad! You don't drink much, do you? Hardly a whole glass out of this. Was it too dry for you?'

'No, I liked it, but I don't drink much.'

'So I see. Two glasses of good wine an evening won't kill you, and the food will taste far better, too. Tell me about your childhood—how many brothers and sisters do you have?'

'One of each.' She cut him a slice of the tart and he poured cream from the small jug on to it.

'Mmm, delicious,' he said, tasting it. 'Older or younger?'

'Sorry?' she asked blankly, staring.

'Your brother and sister.'

'Oh, both older. Guy is thirty-one and married with a baby. Ginny is twenty-six and just got engaged.'

'You like them?'

Startled, she said, 'Of course I'm fond of them!'

He gave her a sardonic look. 'That wasn't what I asked—they're family, so of course you must say you are attached to them, but do you really like them?'

'Yes, I really do,' she insisted. 'Our mother liked to have one baby at a time, she didn't want to have several tiny children to cope with, so she left big gaps between us all, and there was never any jealousy. By the time Ginny arrived, Guy was at school, and by the time I arrived so was Ginny. It worked out well. We've grown up good friends.'

He nodded. 'I had an older sister, when I was small, but she died.'

Christabel sobered, her eyes sympathetic. 'Oh, how sad, I'm sorry. What happened?'

'She caught some childish ailment, it turned into pneumonia, and at that time it was a deadly illness. There was nothing they could do for her; she died. My mother was expecting my brother at the time. She was under such stress that she nearly lost the baby. It was a bad year, that year. I remember it all very clearly.'

'How old were you?' asked Christabel gently, watching him with grave eyes.

'Three.'

'You have a very good memory! I don't remember anything that far back.'

'Perhaps nothing much happened to you when you were three. What happened in my family that year changed everything, even for a three-year-old. My sister vanished, instead I had a baby brother— my mother was ill and strange for months. She seemed to forget all about me.' He was talking in a harsh, low voice, his dark eyes fixed on the glass he was twisting round and round on the table.

'It must have been very disturbing for a three-year-old.' Christabel had never had such traumatic events to cope with, but she could guess at the nightmare that small boy had lived through, and she watched his razor-edged profile with sympathy.

Perhaps that was what had given his writing such depth and emotional power? Such an early experience of tragedy must have had a deep, long-term effect on him. There had been so many deaths in his life, though, hadn't there? First his sister as a child, then his parents when he was barely out of his teens, and later his brother, and his wife. He must at times feel as if he was under some curse!

He looked up, shrugging angrily. 'Let's talk about something else—coffee! How about some coffee?'

'Of course. If you go into the drawing-room, I'll bring it to you.' She got up and began clearing the table, but tonight Roland surprised her by helping. He caught her sideways glance and grinned.

'I usually look after myself in the evening. Jeanne leaves everything ready and I clear away and make my own coffee.' He moved to the stove. 'And I'll do it tonight. You go and sit down and I'll bring the coffee to you.'

She hesitated, having meant to go to bed once she had taken his coffee to him.

'Go on!' he ordered, his tone impatient, peremptory, and his black brows drawing together.

Roland de Bellème was not used to being disobeyed or facing argument.

She wandered around the drawing-room while she waited for him, admiring the paintings on the walls—family portraits, some of them: dark-haired, dark-eyed men and women of the Bellème family, in the clothes of other periods, yet all bearing the same stamp of character and attitude in the arrogant way they stared out of the canvas.

'My ancestors,' Roland said drily as he joined her, carrying the coffee-tray. 'Frightening collection, aren't they?'

'They all look like you,' she said, watching him put the tray down on the low table she had already put in place.

He laughed shortly. 'Thanks.' He poured her coffee, lifted one brow enquiringly. 'Cream? Sugar?'

'Neither, thank you.' She came over to take the cup he held out and he retained his grip on the cup, staring down at her, his eyes narrowed and glittering.

'If I can't find anyone to take care of the children, will you stay and look after them?'

Frowning, she opened her mouth to answer in the negative, but as if guessing that he spoke first, quickly, coaxingly.

'I'll pay very well. I'm sure a student like you can do with some extra money. How much would you say it was worth, a job like that? Name your price.'

'*Monsieur*, I explained why I wanted to go home——' she began uneasily, and he interrupted again, letting go of his side of the coffee-cup so suddenly that she almost dropped her own side.

'I talked to Jeanne this morning while you and the children were out in the field.'

'Oh?' He'd been trying to coax Jeanne into doing what he wanted, had he? Christabel couldn't see him succeeding. Jeanne wouldn't let him bulldoze her into anything. She had known him too long.

'She's taken quite a fancy to them, especially Dani,' he said, and Christabel softened, smiling.

'I know, I'd noticed that. She enjoys teaching Dani how to cook, and Dani loves learning. Dani is at the age when little girls want to stay close to their mother, watching her cooking, and doing housework, copying her, imitating her.'

'And I don't suppose she gets much chance to stay close to Eve-Marie, or learn how to cook and do housework from her?' The dry tone made Christabel frown.

'Well, that isn't her mother's fault! Eve-Marie is a good cook, and she does most of the housework herself. Her home is always immaculate. It's just that Dani is at school all day, and when she comes home Eve-Marie has to leave for the theatre, so Dani doesn't really see too much of her mother during the day.'

'You're very loyal to my sister-in-law,' Roland said, watching her in a way that made her nervous.

'I like her! Don't you?' She put up her chin and eyed him back defiantly, and he grimaced.

'Oh, I've nothing against Eve-Marie, except the way she has landed me with her two brats! As I was saying, Jeanne's attitude to them has altered. She thought they would be nothing but a nuisance, and she's changed her mind. She said she wouldn't mind looking after them——'

'Oh, well, then——' Christabel began in relief, but he cut her short again.

'For a week or two!' He considered Christabel, his black head on one side and his eyes amused by her expression. 'She says she's too old to cope with them for any longer than that. She couldn't possibly do it for the whole summer. So, if anyone answers my advertisement, well and good, you can go back to England at once. But if I can't find anybody else, will you stay for three weeks, and then go to England? You would get some time at home, then, wouldn't you? And Jeanne won't mind looking after them for the rest of the time until their mother gets back.'

Christabel felt trapped, her amber eyes wide and confused. Three whole weeks here? Seeing him every day? Her heart beat inside her with a pace that made her whole body shake. She was afraid, excited, disturbed. She ought to go, get away before... before what? she asked herself, staring into his compelling dark eyes. What was she so scared of?

'What are you so scared of?' he asked her, as if he could read her mind and had picked up the question she was asking herself, and she looked at him dazedly. How had he managed to pick that thought out of the air?

Pulling herself together, she said, 'I'm not scared of anything! It's simply that I was looking forward to getting home. I've been working very hard at my studies. Don't you think I deserve a holiday?'

He shrugged. 'Of course, but can't you have one here? And then go home? Aren't you enjoying yourself?'

'Well, yes, but——'

'Don't you like the *manoir*?'

'Yes, of course I do, it's fascinating, but——'

'I realise there isn't much to do, but I'll show you my part of Brittany whenever I have a few hours free. I'll make the time, take you and the children sightseeing—to see the ancient stones at Carnac, for instance. Far more impressive than Stonehenge, you know. *We* have row upon row of standing stones, hundreds of them.'

'Is it far?'

'Oh, yes, it would take all day to drive there and back, and we'd have to leave very early in the morning. But there are shorter trips. It will be market-day in town in two days' time—I could drive you and the children there to see the market, then you could have lunch and go to the beach for the afternoon. The weather is quite good, you'd all enjoy that, wouldn't you? And around five o'clock, I could pick you up again.' He looked down at her. 'Think how much you would be learning about this part of France!'

Christabel knew it was crazy, sheer madness to give in, but she couldn't resist the charm in his dark eyes, the warmth in his smile.

In bed that night she woke up suddenly from a very real dream, and sat up to find the moonlight on her face and to remember in hot confusion what she had been dreaming. She had not been imagining anything. She had been remembering. Remembering the first night she had come here—those disturbing moments in Roland's arms, the overwhelming power of his body, his suffocating mouth forcing her lips to part, his anger and the threats he had made.

That night he had pushed her away, called her a schoolgirl and looked at her contemptuously—but in her dream it had been different, and she put her hands to her face, closing her eyes and groaning aloud in dismay.

In her dream Roland had not stopped, he had not pushed her away, and she had not fought him or wanted him to stop. She opened her eyes and stared at nothing, her moonlit face shimmering with the muddle of emotions fighting inside her. She should not stay here; she should go home at once!

She didn't, of course, and she knew she wouldn't go even as she was telling herself how wise it would be to leave immediately. She wouldn't go because she couldn't. She could not bring herself to go away and never see Roland again, even though she knew there was no future in the way she had begun to feel.

He was never going to be seriously interested in her. The only reason he had made a pass at her was because he had been so angry over being landed with his nieces. He had wanted to hit someone, and she was the only person around—but he couldn't hit her, she was a female, so he had made love to her in a way which was just as humiliating, just as contemptuous, as any blow would have been.

She wished he had hit her. She could have forgotten that. She knew she would never forget being in his arms, even if he *had* kissed her with dislike and rage.

She lay down again and closed her eyes, emptying her mind of all thought, willing sleep to come—and eventually it did come, but in the morning she was pale and exhausted.

Jeanne Normand noticed at once when she came into the kitchen. 'Oh, you poor thing! What's wrong? Aren't you well?'

'I didn't sleep, that's all.'

'Ah, the moonlight!' Jeanne said, her face knowing.

'It kept me awake half the night,' agreed Christabel ruefully, impressed by Jeanne's guesswork.

'It's dangerous, the moon! It can get inside your head and drive you crazy. Be careful, Bel. You must close your shutters, keep it out.'

Christabel laughed, but Jeanne was utterly serious.

'I mean it! Tonight, close your shutters, and keep them closed until the moon is on the wane.'

'Will Bel turn into a wolf if the moon shines on her?' Dani asked, grinning from ear to ear.

'Don't be silly,' Christabel said. 'Drink your hot chocolate. Jeanne, Monsieur Roland tells me that if I stay on for another three weeks you might be prepared to take over from me for the rest of the holiday. Is that true?'

Jeanne shrugged and set hot coffee and a crisp, flaky croissant in front of her. 'I told him I would, yes. I must be insane, mind you. They'll make me feel my age, and I'm bound to regret it, but I did promise to look after them for part of this holiday, if you would stay for the first half.'

Christabel sighed, her mouth twisting.

Watching her, Jeanne asked softly, 'Did you tell him yes or no?'

'If he can't find anyone to take over from me, I said I'd stay for three weeks.'

Jeanne grinned at her, eyes full of wry fellow-feeling. 'He can coax your soul out of your body, can't he?'

Oh, God, yes, Christabel thought—she couldn't have put it better herself, and a shiver ran down her spine, but she managed to keep any of that off her face, she managed to laugh lightly and shrug.

'Well, he's promised to pay me well, anyway!'

'Good for you!' Jeanne said. 'You hold him to that. It's no easy job, looking after these two wicked children.'

Dani and Nina grinned at that, knowing she did not mean it. They got down from the table and asked eagerly if they might go out now that they'd finished, and Christabel warned them as usual not to go near the horses until she joined them, but she let them go. She wasn't far behind them, in fact. She did not want Jeanne to ask too many questions. The old woman was much too shrewd and saw too much.

Later that day, after a light lunch, Christabel and the children walked through the fields on a journey of exploration, and discovered a secret little cove which they first glimpsed from the cliffs, a beach of whitish sand, some rocks, a semi-circle of cliffs rising sharply up around it. They stood gazing down into it with fascination.

'I wonder if there's a way down?' said Dani.

'I don't see a path,' said Christabel, then frowned anxiously. 'Nina, keep back from the edge! No, children, come away—it's too dangerous to peer down like this, and I don't think there's any way down.'

'Oh, but Bel, it's so pretty!' Nina said, stepping back a little.

'I know, I'm sorry, but we have to get back to the *château* to help Jeanne with the dinner!'

'Yes, come on, never mind the old beach,' said Dani, who adored helping Jeanne in the kitchen, and both little girls tore away through the long, rustling grass.

Christabel was turning away, too, when she saw Roland emerging from somewhere at the foot of the cliffs. He ran down the white sand towards the waves breaking over the wet black rocks, and Christabel froze on the spot, her mouth dry, her eyes wide in shock.

Roland was naked. She should have looked away, but she couldn't; she was riveted by the sight of his lean brown body moving with that matador's grace, a physical arrogance and assurance which compelled admiration. She stood there, staring at the way the deep indentation of his spine made a paler line in his tanned back, his shoulders by contrast deeply gold, his buttocks paler again, his long, muscular legs dark with hair and browned by the sun.

She had never seen a man naked before, and she couldn't take her eyes off him. He was beautiful, intensely sexy. She watched until he had run out into the sea which soon covered him up to the neck. He launched himself into the water, his brown arms moving rhythmically, his black head bobbing up and down on the blue surface, looking like the head of a seal.

At that instant Christabel heard the children shouting for her. 'Bel! Bel! What are you doing?'

Roland must have heard them, too—or perhaps her startled movement on the cliff edge caught his eye?

Whatever the reason, he turned suddenly on to his back and stared upwards, shading his eyes as he floated there on the bright blue sea, his hair slicked back against his scalp.

Her face burning with embarrassment at being caught watching him at that precise moment, Christabel turned and ran.

# CHAPTER SEVEN

CHRISTABEL was very edgy for the rest of the afternoon, afraid of how Roland would look at her when he came to dinner, but when he walked into the kitchen he didn't seem any different. If he had noticed her on the cliff, he had forgotten all about it—or perhaps it simply had had no significance for him?

She wasn't sure whether to be relieved or insulted. She decided on relief as the safer reaction. They ate their evening meal in an amiable way, discussing a whole range of neutral subjects—French art, French poetry, French drama on Christabel's side, and, on Roland's side, farming, the life-cycle of the liver-fluke in sheep, the diseases to which a cow was prevalent, and other fascinating topics.

'Bored?' he asked her with amusement as they were drinking their coffee.

'No, just curious,' she said, lowering her lashes and watching him through them.

His mouth twisted quizzically. 'When you look at me that way you remind me of a mischievous kitten watching a bird she's thinking of catching! Are you thinking of catching me? Because I warn you, I'm too wise a bird to get caught, and curiosity killed the cat—isn't that what they say in England? You see, I do speak some English—enough to get by if I ever have to go there, which, God willing, I never shall again!' He gave her a wry smile and she knew that he was being deliberately provocative to distract her from whatever question she had been about to ask him. She was not deterred, though. The longer she knew him, the more she wanted to know why he had stopped writing.

'Why do you hate talking about your writing?' she asked, and he got up abruptly, took her cup out of her hand, and pulled her to her feet, as though she were a child.

'Bed.'

The curt order, the anger darkening his face, made her obey, but at the door she paused and looked back.

'It helps to talk about things, you know.'

'When I need a psychiatrist, I'll get a professional, thank you.' He sank back into his chair and stared at the ceiling, frowning.

She couldn't leave it like that; she admired his work too much, and couldn't help thinking how marvellous it would be if she could persuade him back to the theatre. Talent like his shouldn't be buried.

'You're such a marvellous writer,' she softly said. 'I told you I've read all your plays, didn't I? And seen some of them. There have been several revivals during the two years I've been in Paris, and I went to all of them.'

He had linked his hands behind his black head and was fixedly gazing up at the ceiling, scowling.

'I don't want to talk about the theatre. I'm out of it, and I'm not interested in going back.'

She stood there watching him, wondering what he was really thinking, and at the same time involuntarily admiring the strong lines of his face,

the deep eye-sockets, the way his hair sprang from
a deep widow's peak on his forehead, the long nose
and hard mouth, the force of the jawline. It was
not a face you could forget easily. She knew it was
going to show up in her dreams for a long time to
come, and that reminded her that she would have
to go home in three weeks. A deep-seated ache
began somewhere inside her and she bit her inner
lip.

What on earth was wrong with her? A couple of
days ago she couldn't wait to get home, she'd been
raging against being trapped here. Now, suddenly,
she caught herself wishing time would slow down
so that the next three weeks should stretch out
forever.

Still staring at the ceiling, Roland asked sharply,
'Was it Eve-Marie who asked you to talk me into
a come-back? Or one of her director friends? Was
it Grandval? Or that swine of a theatre manager,
Claude de Larzac?'

'I told you, nobody asked me to talk to you!'

'And I don't believe you! I've had approaches
before, over the past years. I know the way those
bastards operate, and I know what makes them tick.
Money is their *raison d'être*; nothing else matters,
and my plays make money for them. They don't
give a damn for art! In fact, it's anathema to them.
They don't care why I write, or why I've stopped.
They want to use me as a money-machine, so
they've racked their brains to find ways of getting
me at work again. They've tried everything they
could think of...'

His head shifted and the hostile, sardonic dark
eyes pierced her, his mouth a straight line. 'Do you

think you're the first emissary to arrive? Well, you're not. At first they sent down an actress, someone I'd known quite well years ago. Still a very lovely, very sexy creature, although she's over thirty. She didn't get anywhere, so they tried someone I didn't know, a sexy little blonde around your age. Still no sale.' He smiled coldly and she shivered. 'I suppose it's flattering that they take so much trouble, but they're wasting their time. Go back to Paris and tell them that. Tell them to leave me alone because they won't get anywhere, even by offering me a wide-eyed little schoolgirl.' His insulting gaze wandered over her from head to foot and she tensed, her face burning.

'You're crazy!' she burst out huskily, and he smiled with a cool cruelty that made her back away, trembling.

'No, I'm just not into teaching little girls the rites of love!'

'Don't use that word!' Christabel flung back at him bitterly. 'You don't know what love means.'

'No, maybe I don't,' he agreed icily, his narrowed eyes fixed on her face. 'But I know what it means to want a woman's body, and you're here alone with me, remember. You'd be wise to get out of this room before I decide to take possession of what you've been flaunting in front of me ever since you got here.'

'I haven't been doing anything of the kind!'

'Running about the corridor upstairs wearing nothing but a towel!'

Hot-faced, she couldn't deny it had happened. 'Only once,' she muttered, her eyes sliding away from the dark challenge of his. 'And I didn't expect to see you or I wouldn't have risked it.'

'*No?* And what about this afternoon? I saw you up on the cliffs, watching me.'

She bit down on her lip, her head drooping. 'That was accidental, I didn't realise——'

'I hope you enjoyed what you saw!' he drawled with a sting in his voice, and she hated him, unable to meet his eyes. She didn't hear him move until he was very close to her and her startled, alarmed gaze rose to find him only inches away, smiling with silky menace.

'I'll admit I'm tempted tonight,' he murmured, his dark eyes focused on her quivering, parted lips. 'The nights are always tough.' He put a hand to her face, cupped her chin, stroked her cheek with one long index finger, then ran the finger along the yielding line of her mouth. 'It's that shining innocence,' he said, his lips twisting cynically. 'It's so obvious you've hardly even been kissed, and you blush every time I look at you.'

She was blushing now, and hating him, her amber eyes darkened with a heady mixture of desire and confusion.

'Stop talking as if I were a child!' she muttered, looking away from the mockery of his eyes, then helplessly looked back, at his mouth's cruel sensuality. She didn't want to look at it, she fought against the compulsion, but she was possessed by a strange need to look at him, a yearning to touch him which she had never felt before and couldn't explain even to herself. She didn't touch him, of course. She waited for him to make the first move, hardly breathing, her mouth as dry as a desert.

When his lips at last touched hers she gave a weak sigh, her eyes closing, and without any conscious intention on her part her arms went round his neck. Her hands clutched his hair, the thick, rough strands curling around her fingers while she kissed him back, pulling his head down towards her.

Ever since she had seen him on that beach, running with the grace of some wild animal, his naked brown body gleaming in the sunlight, she had been obsessed with images of him, even though she tried to push them out of her memory.

She had never been in love, never desired a man before; this was all new to her, and she had no real idea how to handle it, how to control the heated instincts governing her. Her head was dizzy and she was barely able to stand as she felt their bodies touching, her small breasts crushed into the muscular wall of his chest, his thigh pushing between her legs, his hands caressing her restlessly, her throat, her shoulders, down the slender line of her back to her buttocks.

'I want you,' he whispered thickly against her yielding mouth. 'God, I want you.'

He lifted his head and framed her flushed face between his palms, watching her eyes slowly open, their pupils huge with excited desire. Roland watched her in silence for a moment, his face rigid again, a bitterness in his face that drained all the heated urgency out of her body.

'Satisfied, now?' he asked her as if he hated her, his voice like the sting of a whip. 'I've admitted I want you, that should do your childish ego a lot of good. You can go back to Paris and tell my sister-in-law that I almost lost my head over you. You almost got there! For a girl who's hardly the new Brigitte Bardot, that's quite a compliment, isn't it?' He gave her a glacial, mocking smile. 'Or does it just mean I'm a starving man who will jump at anything he's offered?'

Tears burned the back of her eyes. She hadn't expected such a vicious insult, and the pain showed in her face.

He frowned, his mouth crooked, pushed her away, moved restlessly on the balls of his feet as if about to break into running. 'God, don't look at me like that, like some trapped little rabbit bleeding to death! You're still such a child, and I keep forgetting that. The way you make me feel and the way you are yourself are so far apart——' He broke off, scowling. 'Look, I'm sorry if that hurt you, I'd no right to insult you... I'm not angry with you so much as my sister-in-law and her friends, who sent you down here. And with myself for wanting to take their bait!' He forced a wry little smile at her. 'But not quite, Bel, *ma belle*. No, I think I'll sleep alone tonight. You must find someone else to introduce you to the rites of love and possession.'

Christabel couldn't get a word out; she turned and ran from the room, crying silently all the way up the broad, sweeping staircase to her bedroom, where she undressed with shaking hands and climbed into bed knowing she had no hope of sleep tonight, her brain on fire with pain and humiliation. She lay awake until she heard Roland come to bed, heard his door close quietly and then silence descend. It did not bring sleep with it, for her, at least. No doubt Roland slept deeply enough!

As usual, he had already eaten and left the house by the time she and the children got downstairs, which was one relief, because it meant she did not have to see him that day until the evening.

She didn't see him at all, as it turned out, because he went out to dinner with the local mayor and did not return until after Christabel was in bed, and so it was not until dinnertime the following day that they actually met again, and that evening they were not alone together because Roland had invited an old friend to have dinner. They did not eat in the kitchen, but in the much grander dining-room, all oak panels and silver candelabra. Jeanne stayed on to serve the meal, and Christabel was not allowed to help her.

'No, tonight you are a guest,' said Jeanne lightly. 'Monsieur Roland has Jean Menez to dinner once every couple of months. They were boys together, you know? Jean farms across the valley. His wife is in hospital having their third child, and his mother-in-law from Nantes has moved in to look after him and the other children, so he is glad to get away for an evening just now! Old Madame Tavers is a scold, no doubt about it. She always comes when Colette Menez is having her babies, and I meet her at market while she's here. Good heavens, how that woman can talk! And all complaints. The fruit here isn't as good as the fruit she can buy at home, the meat is no good, nor is the fish. Nothing is good enough for her! Poor Jean is very patient. I think Monsieur Roland would turn her out of doors if she kept on at him that way!'

'I'm sure he would,' Christabel agreed. She was deeply relieved that she was not going to be left alone with Roland this evening, and ready to be friendly to Jean Menez, whatever he was like!

In fact, she liked him on sight, and somehow in conversation hit upon his pet hobby, local history, which he had been studying since he was a boy, and about which he was genuinely interesting. Christabel's motive in getting him to talk so much was originally to stop any awkward silences between herself and Roland, but soon she was fascinated by what Jean Menez was telling her.

He was a man of around forty, short, sturdily built, with a round, bullet head and dark hair, brown eyes and an olive skin. It was clear that he and Roland were very good friends. They had a great deal in common, of course—both farmers, both from local families of many generations, both interested in history and reading.

Christabel wondered how Jean felt about Roland's plays and his baffling abandonment of his career in the theatre. Under Roland's eyes she did not dare ask Jean, however, and the subject never came up.

'Have you been to our local market?' Jean asked her. 'There's a fascinating little antiques stall there, and you can buy some excellent local pottery.'

'I haven't been yet, but I'm hoping to go,' she said without looking at Roland, and he took the hint.

'I intend to drive her and the children into town next market-day,' he said drily.

He kept his word, taking them to town so that they could visit the market, and leaving them there to have lunch and shop. It was a hot, sunny, windless day, not a cloud in the sky. The market was delightful, crowded with farmers and their wives as well as townspeople and some tourists. Christabel bought some of the local *chèvre*—little round goat's cheeses, with herbs pressed into the outer skin—and local fruit—cherries and strawberries—which the children immediately began to eat as they followed her around the stalls. She bought presents for her family, too: a square of yellowy ivory Breton lace for Ginny which might be perfect as a wedding veil; a piece of local pottery for her mother's collection; a handmade cherrywood pipe for her father; and for her brother Guy and his wife a green glass vase from the antique stall. It was not very old and not very valuable, so it wasn't expensive, but it was very pretty and she knew they would like it. The children bought presents for their mother, too, so that by the time they all went to lunch they were carrying a large rush basket of little parcels.

After lunch they went down to the beach and swam and sunbathed until Roland came to pick them up again. They climbed into the car, flushed with sunshine, gritty with sand, their hair tousled, their eyes drowsy.

'I don't need to ask if you had a good day!' said Roland as he drove off.

'We had a lovely day,' Christabel said, so happy that she smiled at him unselfconsciously for the first time in days. 'Did you have any luck?'

'Luck?' He looked blankly at her.

'You were going to call in at the newspaper office to see if you had had any replies to the advertisement.'

'Oh, that!' he said, looking ahead at the road. 'No. No luck. But you said you would stay on for three weeks, didn't you? So, there's no problem.'

'I was still hoping that——'

'Well, I'm afraid you hoped in vain,' he interrupted, looking impatient. 'Nobody wants the job.' The car put on speed up the cliff road towards the *Manoir du Sorcier*, and Christabel watched the late afternoon sun sinking behind it, giving it a blood-red halo, sinister, disturbing.

'I wonder what he was like...' she thought aloud, and Roland shot her a glance sideways.

'Who?'

'The sorcerer.'

'The...?' His brows rose and he laughed. 'Oh, him.'

'Yes, your ancestor! I wonder if you're like him?'

It had been a joke, she was laughing, teasing him, completely at ease—and then suddenly she saw his face and stopped laughing. Roland was rigid, his features harsh and taut with menace.

'I don't find that funny!' he snarled, eyes like black ice, his jaw set angrily.

'I... It was a joke!' She stammered because she was taken aback, baffled by another of his abrupt changes of mood. You never knew where you were with him. He was as unpredictable as a caged panther, liable to spring at you without warning.

'My sister-in-law did gossip to you, didn't she?' he muttered, keeping his voice down because the children sat in the back seats. Frowning, he leaned forward and turned on the radio, letting the insistent beat of a French pop song flood the car so that the children should not hear what he was saying above the noise of the music.

'I don't know what you're talking about!' she protested, and he snarled at her, his lip curling viciously.

'Don't lie to me!'

'I'm not lying!'

She might as well have saved her breath; he wasn't listening. 'It's as clear as crystal that you know something of what happened, and being a female you'd like to know more! Well, I'm not in need of a confidante, I've no intention of telling you a single thing, so stop trying to worm the story out of me! If you drop any more hints or make any more of your little jokes, you'll regret it.'

He put his foot down and the car roared forward, making her fall back into her seat, her head hitting the edge of the window. She was too alarmed by the speed with which he was driving to say anything, and Roland was silent for the rest of the way, his profile dark and brooding, his knuckles white as he gripped the steering-wheel.

He dropped them at the drawbridge and they went straight upstairs to have a bath and go to bed. The children weren't hungry; they had eaten a *croque-monsieur* at a café on the beach while they waited for Roland. They loved the toast with cheese and ham on top, but Christabel was not so keen, and had refused to have any.

'What's the matter with Roland tonight?' asked Dani as Christabel tucked them into bed. 'He's got a terrible temper, hasn't he?'

'Terrible,' said Christabel, smiling as if it were all a big joke, although she felt more like crying.

'Now, you go to sleep, darlings. See you in the morning.'

They were tired after their day out, especially all that walking around the town followed by an afternoon on the beach. The combination of sea-air and sun had made them very sleepy. She could see that they were almost asleep already.

She hesitated on the landing. She felt sleepy herself, and she wasn't hungry. She was tempted to go to bed.

No! she thought. Face it! You're tempted to keep out of Roland's way, that's the truth, isn't it? And that's just cowardice. Running away is never the answer.

She showered and changed and went down to serve dinner. As always, there was no sign of Roland until dead on seven o'clock, when she heard him coming down from his own bedroom. Christabel tensed, fighting to appear calm.

She needn't have worried. When he walked into the kitchen she saw at once that he did not intend to continue with that bitter attack on her. He was calm, rather quiet, perhaps, but they ate the meal in a civilised atmosphere, each of them careful to stick to neutral subjects. She said what wonderful weather they were having, and Roland talked about the forest fires currently blazing along the Côte d'Azur; Christabel said the market had been fascinating, and told him what she had bought. Roland said she must go again next week, and she said she would like to.

'And maybe at the weekend you'd like to drive to Carnac, as I promised?'

'Oh, I'd be delighted!' she said eagerly. 'You haven't got a book on the stones, have you?'

'Several. I'll find one for you,' he promised, and after they had cleared the table and washed up he suggested that she might like to come up to his tower-study to choose a book on Carnac.

She was surprised by the invitation, but discreetly hid that, following him up the winding stairs to the room she had visited before. Roland walked along the shelves, picking out a book here, another there.

'I collect topography,' he said in French, and she did not recognise the last word and gazed blankly at him, so he laughed and said it in very good English.

'That's a new word to me, I must remember it,' she said, and he nodded.

'Your French is usually so good I find it hard to believe you're English.'

She went slightly pink with pleasure. 'Thank you.'

He smiled at her, his dark eyes amused and gentle. 'Not at all. Here you are, these two are the best books on Carnac. Like Stonehenge, Carnac attracts its share of lunatics and extremists, and some books that get published are completely crazy, full of wild theories, but these two will give you a down-to-earth account of who probably erected the stones and why they were put up.'

She took the books and felt his fingers touch her own; her pulses went far wilder than any of the theories about Carnac that he had been mocking. If Roland guessed how he made her feel, would he mock her, too?

Clutching the books, she backed towards the door. 'Well, goodnight, thank you,' she stammered, and Roland watched her with a strange, abstracted expression, as though he was thinking of something else and was not aware of her at all.

'Goodnight,' he murmured, and she felt like shouting at him, throwing the books at him—anything to get his attention, make him as conscious of her as she always was of him.

But she could imagine his stunned expression if she did! So she controlled the impulse, fixing a stupid, blank smile on her face as she left. In her own room she sat on the bed and looked down at the books. They were probably going to be very boring, but at least if she read them in bed with any luck they would soon send her off to sleep.

Roland couldn't take them to Carnac that weekend because the weather changed overnight, and on the Saturday morning rain fell in a relentless downpour which continued all day. The children moped around, staring wistfully out at the horses, so Christabel organised games for them, which at least kept them occupied all morning, and in the afternoon Jeanne made biscuits with them. They ate most of what they made at teatime, and then Roland offered to take them all into town to see a film at the local cinema.

It was a very successful evening, and the children sang happily all the way home. The following day the weather was changeable: showers one minute, sun the next. Roland said that it would be best to postpone the trip to Carnac until the following weekend, which was disappointing for Christabel, but at least the children were able to ride for an hour, and later that afternoon Roland took them all for a drive into town to the hospital, so that he could visit Madame Menez to congratulate her on the birth of a son, whom she had decided to call Roland Jean.

Leaving the two children with Jean Menez in the corridor, Roland insisted on taking Christabel to meet Colette Menez.

Colette was in her late twenties, a petite, dark woman with delicate features and huge, soulful eyes. She looked pale and tired, but she was obviously delighted by her son, who slept in a swinging basket by his mother's bed.

Christabel was shy at first, but gradually she relaxed as she realised that Colette was friendly and ready to like her, especially after Christabel had enthusiastically admired the baby.

'For some crazy reason, she actually likes children,' Roland drily said, and Colette looked quickly at him, then at Christabel, smiling.

'And they like her, which shows better taste,' said Roland, and Christabel blushed, taken aback by the compliment. Colette was watching them curiously, her eyes thoughtful.

'Stop teasing her! He's a monster, Christabel, but don't let him scare you off. He's not as black as the Bellème legend paints all his ancestors!'

'Aren't I, then?' asked Roland with a wicked gleam in his dark eyes, and Colette wagged a finger at him.

'Behave yourself! What must Christabel think of you? What a lovely name you have, Christabel, but it is rather long. Do you have a pet name?'

'Bel,' Roland said. 'They call her Bel.'

Christabel looked away, biting her inner lip because any woman hearing that name and taking a look at her face was going to want to laugh. She was no beauty, and she wished her parents had given her some other name—something plain and everyday to suit her appearance.

Colette didn't laugh, though, or give her face a disbelieving look. 'May I call you Bel, then? That's much easier to say,' was all she said, and Christabel gave her a shy, grateful look and nodded. From that moment she was sure she liked Colette.

When they left shortly after that, Colette said, 'I do hope I'll see you again before you go back to England, Bel. Roland, you must bring her to see me again.'

'I will,' he promised.

In the car, she said, 'You have nice friends. Both Jean and Colette are charming.'

'That's why they're my friends,' Roland said, his face stiff and his voice flat. 'I learnt through bitter experience to pick my friends wisely. At one time I'd rush into a relationship without looking too closely at the other person, whether it was a man or a woman—but not now!'

Christabel watched him through lowered lashes, wishing she dared ask him what bitter experience had made him so wary and so cynical—yet knowing that if she risked even an oblique question he would turn hostile in a second and close up like a clam.

Dani suddenly said in the silence that followed, 'Nina feels sick!' and Roland pulled up abruptly to let Nina get out. Christabel scrambled out after her and gently wiped her pale face with a damp tissue, soothing her, after the little girl threw up in the ditch. Roland watched them both, frowning. After a few minutes Nina felt well enough to get back into the car.

'I hope she isn't sickening for something nasty,' Roland said, and from the back seat Dani answered him.

'No, she just ate too many sweets while we were waiting for you. Jean gave us each a bag of sweets and Nina ate all hers.'

'Oh, Nina!' Christabel said in gentle reproof. 'That wasn't very sensible, was it? No wonder you were sick. You won't do that again, will you?'

'And you wonder why I didn't want them here!' said Roland, driving on to the *Manoir du Sorcier*. 'Children are nothing but trouble!'

The following week seemed to pass in a flash. The spell of bad weather ended, the sunshine returned and Christabel saw to it that the children were out of doors as much as possible. They rode each morning, then took a walk with Caesar, to whom they had become very attached once he had accepted them and become friendly. He enjoyed his walks and so did the little girls, who had always wanted to have a dog of their own.

Several days that week Roland drove them into town to spend an afternoon on the beach—swimming, sailboarding, playing beach games, but mostly just sunbathing. They lay stretched out on mattresses under the striped beach-umbrellas and read, or dozed, listening to music on their personal tape players, each wearing headphones and dreamy expressions, as if they had suddenly turned into androids. Those days were tranquil, a blissful existence of sun and sea.

Christabel kept a wary eye on the children and made sure that their exposure to the sun was gradual and carefully regulated, and was herself careful not to spend too long in the sun.

Roland commented one afternoon, when he picked them up at the beach, on her sun-ripened skin. 'You're getting a tan!' He gave her a long, thoughtful stare. 'You look quite different. It suits you.'

'Thank you,' she said, prickling with irritation because he sounded both surprised and amused.

'You look far healthier than you did when you first arrived. You were a pallid town child two weeks ago—all skin and bone. Now you have a bloom you didn't have before; the sun and sea-air, I suppose. You're filling out, too—you've acquired a few female curves from somewhere.'

A strange weakness spread through her and she looked down, her lashes brushing her cheeks. Roland drove on, but occasionally threw her another of his sideways looks.

'Obviously, you've been working too hard in Paris,' he said after a pause. 'If I were you, I wouldn't burn the candle at both ends again next year. You have enough to do just passing your exams. Don't let my sister-in-law use you as a nursery-maid every night.'

She frowned, putting a hand on his knee without thinking, and whispered, 'Shh...the children are listening!' He threw a glance back at them, then looked down at her hand, his mouth twisting.

She snatched it away, as scarlet as if she had been dipped in hot water, and stared fixedly out of the car window for the rest of the way. He dropped them off and went on to garage the car while she took the children to their room, read them a story, and took her time in showering and changing before very reluctantly going down to dinner. She didn't feel much like facing Roland again tonight. Why did he always make her feel as if she were about to face a firing squad?

Roland was not in the kitchen, but Jeanne was, grumbling as Christabel appeared, 'I began to think you'd gone to bed and wouldn't be down for dinner!'

'You shouldn't have waited!' Christabel said, surprised to see her still there. 'You know I can cope with serving dinner by myself! You should have gone home—off you go now, I'll do everything.' She was very sorry she had delayed Jeanne: it had been thoughtless of her when she knew how far the old woman had to cycle home.

'Oh, I would have gone, but I had to see you first. I'm afraid you'll be dining alone tonight. Monsieur has had to go out; Gaston's son has had an accident and Monsieur is driving them into town. He probably won't be back for dinner. He said that as he was going back into town he might as well eat at a restaurant and drive Gaston and his wife back here once little Yves is settled in the hospital. Luckily it's quiche and salad, so what you don't eat will keep in the fridge until tomorrow. Will you start with terrine? Or——'

'I'm not hungry,' Christabel said blankly, her mind in turmoil. 'The quiche and salad will be more than enough, thank you, Jeanne.'

'Well, as you like! Would you like me to stay with you until Monsieur gets back? Don't be afraid to say so. I know this place can be quite scary after dark, when you're all on your own here.'

'No, I wouldn't dream of it! I'm not frightened. Of course not! You go on home, Jeanne.'

Jeanne shrugged. 'Oh, well, it's up to you! Goodnight, then, Bel. Monsieur shouldn't be too late.'

'I'll be fine, don't worry.'

'I'll leave Caesar with you for company, shall I?'

'Yes, do that,' she said, smiling, because she was becoming quite fond of the great hound. He looked and sounded much fiercer than he was; at times she thought his master was like that too—and then Roland would turn hostile dark eyes on her and his face would ice up, and she'd feel the same fear of him she had felt the night she arrived.

Alone in the kitchen that evening, she had Caesar with her, lying near her feet, his huge head on his paws and his eyes almost closed, yet always ready to open wide at a sound from her.

'I wish you could talk,' she said to him, and the dog lifted his head to stare searchingly at her. 'I'm sure you know your master better than anyone else does! You could tell me what he's really like, couldn't you?'

Caesar wagged his tail obligingly, but with a puzzled expression. What was she talking about? his eyes asked.

'Never mind, go back to sleep!' she laughed, clearing the table while the dog watched. After a while Caesar gave a deep sigh and put his head on his paws again, closing his eyes.

When she had finished tidying the kitchen, Christabel urged the dog out into the hall to stand guard until Roland returned. 'I'm off to bed,' she told him, turning towards the stairs, but as her foot touched the bottom stair she heard the sound of a car on the cliff road and her heart leapt. Was that Roland coming back early? She glanced quickly at her watch; it was not yet nine o'clock, but perhaps Roland had decided not to have dinner in town, and had come back home to have a late supper here instead.

Would he be expecting her to be there to cook it for him? She dithered at the foot of the stairs, unable to make up her mind whether to run away and avoid seeing him tonight—or to wait until he came in case he did want a meal.

Of course, he could cook it for himself—she knew from Jeanne that he was perfectly capable of making a meal and had often done so in the past.

But he must be tired. He had had a long day— longer than usual. He had been up at dawn to work on the farm, and had put in a hard day before driving down to the town to pick up her and the children, only to find, when he returned to the *manoir*, that he would have to drive back to town with the injured child and Gaston and his wife.

She couldn't leave him to cook his own meal at this time of night, after doing all that. She slowly turned back again, knowing that she was going to wait for him—but why was he taking so long to garage the car? It was five minutes since she'd heard the car arriving; where had he got to?

At that moment, someone knocked on the great front door. The sound boomed through the house. Christabel nearly jumped out of her skin. Caesar scrambled to his feet, head back, baying, his black lip curled back from his fanglike teeth.

Roland wouldn't knock at the front door! He would come in, as he most usually did, through one of the side doors. But if it wasn't Roland, who on earth could it be? Why should anyone call here at this time of night?

She wasn't sure whether or not to answer the knock. Had that been Roland's car she had heard? Or had it been someone else's car on the cliff road? She hadn't been worried about it until that moment, but suddenly she became aware of the emptiness of the old house, the echoes of knocking dying away somewhere in the shadows.

There was nobody within earshot if she screamed! she realised. The nearest house was Gaston's cottage, across several fields. Oh, don't be so stupid! Don't start imagining things! she crossly told herself. Why should the caller be dangerous? It was probably someone perfectly respectable— Jean Menez, for instance. Or the Mayor, Roland's friend. Or...

Whoever it was knocked again and Caesar's baying redoubled. 'Shh...down, boy!' Christabel said, moving reluctantly now. The dog sank on to his haunches, watching her, then got up and padded behind her, and she didn't order him back. It was comforting to have him there. Most people would think twice about tackling the huge animal; he was quite a reassuring bodyguard.

She grasped the heavy iron ring of the door and slowly turned it to peer out. It wasn't yet dark; twilight gave the sky a gentle mistiness shot through with rose and gold from the sinking sun. Against that soft light stood a man's shape. Her eyes flashed to his face and she gave a little gasp of mingled relief and surprise, because she had seen that face before.

She knew this man by name and sight, although he probably wouldn't remember her. It was Claude de Larzac, a brilliant actor-director, who ran what was perhaps the most admired theatre in Paris at that time. His company was avant-garde, both in the plays it performed and the way it performed them. Claude de Larzac usually took the best parts himself, and played them with superb skill; nobody disputed that.

Eve-Marie had once introduced Christabel to him at a theatrical party given in Eve-Marie's flat. He had barely glanced at her; he had been much more interested in Eve-Marie. Christabel had wondered if they were lovers, but if they were it was a very discreet affair.

She stared at him now, though, with a rapid succession of reactions—that first relief giving way to puzzled bewilderment, and then to suspicion and wariness, her amber eyes wide and searching.

What was he doing here?

# CHAPTER EIGHT

'DON'T just stand there staring! I'm not a ghost!' he drawled in his famous, smoky voice which would be instantly recognised by anyone in France. 'Can I come in? Or are you going to make me wait out here while you go and tell Roland I want to see him?'

'He isn't at home,' muttered Christabel, and Claude de Larzac's very thin, flyaway eyebrows rose steeply.

'How original! But allow me to tell you that you do not play that line very convincingly. You're blushing and you look the picture of guilt.' He raised his voice, speaking past her into the hall. 'Come on, Roland! I know you're here. Don't be a bastard. I've driven down from Paris this afternoon and I'm badly in need of a drink. You aren't going to turn me away this time, damn you!'

The echoes of that very individual voice came back to them from the empty house and she shivered. Her friends at the Sorbonne would envy her like mad if they knew she was here with Claude de Larzac, listening to that voice as it rang around the great hall.·

'He's dining out this evening,' she said, and Claude looked back at her, his mouth twisting. He was a distinguished man in his late forties, rather smaller than he seemed on stage, slightly built, handsome, with silvery threads in his black hair, and more lines on his face than ever showed in his photographs.

'In that case...' he said softly, and before she knew what was happening he was inside the house, having slid past her like an eel. She spun on her heel to face him, and he put out a casual hand to slam the great front door shut. The crash echoed around them, making her jump.

'I can't invite you in—' she burst out, her voice rising, her eyes worried. 'Please leave, you'll have to see Monsieur de Bellème tomorrow.'

Caesar growled deep in his throat and moved up beside her, his ears back and his body poised for the spring. Claude de Larzac looked down at him, then said crisply, 'Sit!'

To Christabel's fury, the dog sat, and Claude negligently rubbed a hand over his ears, murmuring to him, 'Good boy, well done.'

Caesar looked pleased with himself. Christabel eyed him with disgust. 'Call yourself a watchdog?' she said crossly. 'You're no protection at all, are you?'

'Dogs have good instincts,' Claude drawled. 'He knows I mean you no harm.'

'I wish I did.'

Claude smiled at her. 'I'm sure you know that perfectly well.' He strolled away, looking around him. 'Some place Roland has, isn't it?'

Christabel followed him, agitated by the realisation that if Roland returned and found him here with her he would fly into one of his black tempers. 'Please leave, I can't——'

'How are the children?' he interrupted.

'They're OK!' She was brusque; did he think she was a servant; someone Roland had asked to look after Eve-Marie's children? She was sure he didn't recognise her. Last time they had met he had scarcely glanced at her.

'Will you make me some coffee and sandwiches, Bel?' he asked, and her eyes widened in disbelief. He laughed aloud. 'You have a very expressive face—have you ever thought of going on the stage? Although it's in close-up that you would score. You don't need to use words at all. Your eyes talk.'

'I didn't think you remembered me.'

'Evidently, but why shouldn't I? We met at Eve-Marie's apartment and you are the English girl who lodges with her. See? I remember everything, and I even knew you were staying here.' His dark eyes gleamed. 'In fact, it was my idea.'

Christabel stared fixedly. 'What was?'

'That you should bring the children to Roland.' He wandered away, opening doors, looking and walking on, and Caesar padded after him. 'Is this the way to the kitchen? What a maze of rooms and corridors. I'm dying for some coffee and food.' He gave her an appealing look. 'Anything will do. Bread and cheese, cold meat, some fruit— anything!'

Christabel moved like an automaton: put the light on in the kitchen, began making coffee, offered him a slice of the quiche in the fridge, and made him a little salad.

What exactly had he meant by saying that it had been his idea that she should bring the children to Roland? And what was he doing here?

She had put down all Roland's accusations about a conspiracy as some sort of crazy delusion. Now she began to wonder—what if Roland was right? What if she had been sent down here as part of some plot to get him back to work in the theatre? A flush rose in her face; how crazy could you get? Why on earth would they have sent *her*, of all people? They would have picked someone with more sex appeal, obviously! They had enough out-of-work actresses around who would have jumped at the chance to get to know Roland de Bellème! No, Claude de Larzac could not have meant that. It was too far-fetched.

Claude looked around the kitchen, wrinkling his nose. 'I would rather not eat in here! Bring my supper along and we'll find somewhere more civilised.' He was gone before she could protest, and she had no choice but to run after him, carrying the tray on which she had placed his food and coffee. She found him in the drawing-room, standing by the drinks cabinet, one of Roland's beautiful, hand-cut glass decanters in his hand, pouring himself a glass of Roland's brandy, the one he saved for special occasions.

'You can't drink that!' she broke out huskily, frowning. 'Please, put that down. Monsieur de Bellème will be furious!'

'Roland doesn't frighten me,' Claude said, then sat down, and swirled the brandy round and round, warming the glass with his cupped hand while he inhaled. 'Mmm...beautiful! Well, tell me, little Bel, how are you and Roland getting on?'

She bit her lip, watching him angrily. Roland was going to blame her for this, for letting Claude de

Larzac invade his house, eat his food, drink his brandy. But could she stop him? He was an important man, used to his own way; he had no intention of taking notice of anything she said. She was just a university student and, although he was being perfectly polite, almost amiable, he wouldn't take her seriously. She looked at her watch with anxiety. 'Please, Monsieur de Larzac—I really think you ought to be going soon. Could you please hurry?'

'Oh, but I'm going to wait for Roland,' he drawled, picking up his plate and beginning to eat the quiche. 'Ah, excellent cooking! Did you make this?'

'No, Monsieur de Bellème's housekeeper did.' Christabel's voice was abstracted; she was wondering how she was going to persuade him to leave before Roland returned.

'I vaguely remember some old woman who was here when I last came,' said Claude frowning thoughtfully. 'Is it still the same one? You can't get people like that in Paris, and if you find one they never stay, but life's different in the country, I suppose. And this is the back of beyond! How Roland can stand it, I'll never know. It would drive me crazy in five minutes.' He had finished his brandy and almost finished the quiche; he picked up his coffee and took a mouthful, staring at her over the rim of the cup.

She was uneasy under that shrewd, bright gaze—what was he thinking? 'I rather like it here,' she said defiantly, and he put down his cup, smiling oddly.

'I'm delighted to hear it!' He grinned at her, triumph glittering in his face. 'I told Eve-Marie that Roland would never turn you away, and I was right. The minute I set eyes on you I knew you were the one person he'd allow over the threshold.'

She stared at him, dumbfounded; her heart beat faster. Surely he hadn't thought Roland would like her on sight? 'Why?' she whispered.

He shrugged. 'Don't take this the wrong way, Bel, I mean it as a compliment, I assure you. I chose you because you're... well, let's say very young and sweet. I knew he'd feel quite safe having you under his roof, whereas if Eve-Marie had sent the children here with one of her friends he would have slammed the door in their faces, the way he has before. Roland is sick of sophisticated women. I'm sure Eve-Marie explained why.'

'She didn't explain anything!' burst out Christabel resentfully. 'I only realised that I was owed an explanation after I got here and found that the situation was a lot more complicated than she had told me. For a start, Monsieur de Bellème wasn't expecting me or the children. That has put me in a very difficult situation, and I don't understand why she lied to me about things.'

'She wasn't very happy about having to keep you in the dark,' he soothed. 'Eve-Marie is very fond of you.'

'She has a funny way of showing it!'

'She didn't mean you any harm, you should know her better than that. She had the best of intentions.'

'She wanted to get away to Martinique and couldn't find anyone else to look after her children, you mean!'

'That was part of it,' he admitted with a casual wave of the hand which infuriated Christabel. 'It was an important part for Eve-Marie, you must see that.'

'It was important to me to get away to see my family.'

'You know you'll see them soon, anyway,' he told her impatiently. 'But for Eve-Marie a chance like this film might not come again. She isn't a girl of twenty, remember! She's been around for years now, and she's desperately fighting to establish herself before it's too late.'

Christabel bit her lip, recognising that as the truth, plain and unvarnished, and feeling sorry for Eve-Marie; understanding her, too, in a way she never had before.

Watching her, Claude said softly, 'She grabbed her chance with both hands, and she used you to do it, but can't you understand why she did it? Can't you forgive her?'

'I suppose so,' Christabel said slowly, grimacing.

'Good girl. Eve-Marie is a fine woman, you know. She's had some tragic experiences, and she came through them without ever letting anyone know how much she suffered.'

Christabel guessed he was talking about Hilaire de Bellème, and stared at him intently. 'She rarely talks to me about the past, but I've guessed a little.'

'Has Roland talked to you?' He stared back at her, his eyes narrowed, probing her face. 'Eve-Marie and I often talk about him, about the waste of the last seven years.'

'It's very sad,' Christabel gently agreed. 'I admire his work, too, Monsieur de Larzac. I've tried to talk to him about it, but he just gets angry and walks away or changes the subject.'

'You know why he left Paris?' Claude de Larzac was watching her closely, his face enigmatic. She looked back at him blankly, wondering what he was thinking.

'Because his wife died...'

He shook his head, mouth twisting. 'Too simple, my dear. Death a man gets over, in time—but betrayal cuts deeper. His wife was unfaithful to him right from the start. She was discreet, at first; nobody could say she flaunted her affairs. There were whispers, after a while, rumours one couldn't pin down—but she was a very successful actress. Anyone famous is the object of that sort of gossip— it could all have been mere fantasy.' He smiled cynically. 'Only it wasn't. It was all true. Any number of men, I gather, although Roland didn't know about any of it until he found her diary and the evidence was all there, names, dates, details.'

'I don't want to hear about it!' she muttered, turning away, her stomach cramped.

'You said Eve-Marie never told you anything. And I agree, it's time you knew what this is all about. You know about the accident, I suppose?'

'I don't want to!' She was appalled by what she had already heard. No wonder Roland had become so bitter and cynical; no wonder he had shut himself away in his old family home, and turned his back on the theatre and Paris, all of that over-sophisticated, corrupt world which had betrayed him.

'It was the final act of the tragedy.' Claude de Larzac's mouth writhed in a distasteful pretence of a smile. 'His wife no longer got quite such a kick out of her love affairs, it seems. She needed something more thrilling to give her a kick. She seduced his brother.'

Christabel closed her eyes, white to her hairline. So her wild guesswork hadn't been so beyond belief, after all!

'They went away together one weekend. Hilaire was supposed to be in Lyons on business, and she told Roland that she was flying over to London for a society wedding. In fact, they spent the weekend in a hotel in the Alps. There was a fire during the night. She was killed.'

Christabel flinched, trying to shut out his relentless voice. So that was how Roland's wife had died!

'It was the smoke that killed her, they said at the inquest. Hilaire wasn't killed, but he was badly burned. He took months to die. Eve-Marie had a very bad time; she had the two babies and so she couldn't work, and there was no money coming in. Roland was generous, I have to say that for him. He had every reason for hating Hilaire, but although he would never go to see him in the hospital he made sure Eve-Marie was financially secure. He took care of all expenses for his brother, and for Eve-Marie and the children.'

'Yet he knew by then...' Christabel was overwhelmed.

'He knew, of course, but I don't think he really blamed Hilaire for what had happened. He knew who was to blame.'

'He...he hadn't known until then, though?' She was struggling to imagine how Roland must have felt when he'd found out. The shock must have been appalling—a blow to his self-respect that must have knocked him off his feet.

'He'd found the diary, by then. He showed it to Eve-Marie and told her that the affair had all been his wife's fault. He was sorry for his brother, in fact; by then it was clear that Hilaire wasn't going to pull through. He was in a lot of pain, poor fellow, and eaten up with guilt about his own wife, not to mention Roland.' Claude sighed, frowning. 'It was a pity he hadn't died in the fire, in a way. He paid a heavy price for an affair I don't think he ever truly wanted. He was just weak. Before he died, Roland did see him, just once, and forgave him. Eve-Marie told me. Roland made Eve-Marie an allowance from the royalties of his plays, and then he left Paris and hasn't been back since.'

'You can understand why!' she broke out hoarsely, icy-cold with sick distaste for what she had heard.

'Of course,' Claude agreed, his voice too smooth, too glib. She stared, realising that he might have some surface understanding of how a man would react in such bitter circumstances, but he couldn't imagine how deep the wound might be. He might see the blood, but he could not feel the pain.

'And I've waited patiently,' he added with a charming smile. 'Sure that he would come back to Paris, to where he belongs—the theatre!'

'Your theatre!' she accused and he shrugged, indifferent to her opinion, and assured of his own worth.

'Who discovered him? Who put on his first play? Who has encouraged his every step?' He spread his arms, a gesture of utter certainty. 'Me! Of course he belongs in my theatre. I waited, with all the patience of Job, but he didn't come!'

'So you started trying to lure him up to Paris with pretty women?' she said scornfully. 'And it didn't work.'

Claude looked sharply at her. 'He told you that? Well, well—now that *is* interesting! So he has been talking to you? I wonder what he said?' He considered her, his head to one side. 'Will you tell me?' Before she could angrily refuse, he smiled. 'No, you won't. Well, never mind, I'll tell you. My big seduction scenes didn't work. Perhaps the girls I sent reminded him of his wife. They were both actresses, and not very good ones, I suppose. I didn't manage to move him an inch, and then I met you at Eve-Marie's, and I remembered the legend of the unicorn.'

Blankly, she stared at him. 'What legend?'

'You don't know it?' His brows curved into arches. 'You must have seen the famous French tapestry of the unicorn and the virgin?'

She was still thinking about Roland, an ache centred around her heart. She wished her first romantic notion had been the true explanation, and he was still grieving for a dead, beloved wife. That would have been a much more bearable reason for his pain. He might have got over his grief in time and learnt to love again, but how could he ever be persuaded to trust another woman, let alone love one?

'Are you listening?' Claude said drily. 'You know that a unicorn is a magical white beast like a horse, but with one horn in the middle of its forehead? It is very shy and wary and stays hidden in the darkest part of the forest. If you try to catch it, so the legend goes, it turns wild and destructive, and will even kill. But there is a way to catch a unicorn—you send a virgin into the forest, alone, all in shining white, and she sits down under a tree and sings, and, once it is sure she is a virgin and alone, the unicorn comes and kneels down in front of her and puts its head in her lap.'

Christabel flinched. 'And then, I suppose, men like you come with nets and catch it, poor thing?'

'Something like that.' Claude shrugged, unashamed, indeed slightly amused by the picture.

'That's horrible!' she accused, her eyes hating him. He smiled at her blandly, unaffected by her hostility.

'Maybe, but that's the way to catch a unicorn—and I thought it might be the way to catch Roland, too.'

Roland had rejected the beautiful, sophisticated women they had sent down from Paris to lure him back to the theatre—and so they had picked her out, to trap him for them, as the unicorn was trapped by the virgin. Christabel was humiliated by their reasoning. She wasn't beautiful or sophisticated. She was just young, naïve, inexperienced, and, as they had shrewdly guessed, a virgin. Roland wouldn't suspect that she might try to seduce him. They had been sure that it would be obvious to him that she wouldn't know where to start.

She hated Claude's knowing smile, his cynically amused eyes. It made her sick to know that he had speculated with Eve-Marie as to her sexual status—

a virgin? Or not? She swallowed on a vile taste and
turned away.

'Would you mind going, monsieur?' she said bitterly. 'I've no idea when Monsieur de Bellème will
be home, I want to go to bed, and I can't leave you
down here alone. How do I know you won't steal
the silver and vanish?'

He laughed out loud, his eyes mocking. 'You're
angry with me! You must be very angry or you
wouldn't be so rude! You're such a nicely brought-
up English girl. What do they say in England? A
young lady? So you must be very angry with me.
That's too bad. Did I hurt your feelings? I'm sorry,
I didn't mean to upset you. Don't be touchy, there's
a good girl. When you're my age, you'll realise that
youth and lack of experience is something to envy,
not resent.' He sighed dramatically. 'What I
wouldn't give to be a piece of blank paper again—
for life to write on! But I'm a very crumpled,
scribbled over, grubby piece of paper now, I'm
afraid.' He gave her a coaxing smile.

'If you're expecting me to argue, don't, because
I won't!' she snapped, and he laughed again.

'Well, I am sorry if I hurt your feelings. I
shouldn't have told the truth. There's a moral in
that, isn't there? If I'd lied, you wouldn't be furious
with me now, and with someone my own age I
would have been lying, and they would have been
delighted to hear my lies. It is only the young who
are insulted by being told they're young. The rest
of us long to believe we still have dew on us!'

Christabel moved crossly to the door, unmoved
by his rueful apologies. 'Would you leave now,
please?' She did not like him; he was cynical, a ma-

nipulator, a man without scruple, and he had made her feel like some pathetic pawn in a complex game in which she had no stake. She must get rid of him before Roland got back.

He got up, following her out into the hall, but before she could open the front door he caught hold of her hand and detained her.

Christabel looked up, startled, trying to free herself. 'What now?'

He gently caressed her cheek with one hand. 'Will you tell Roland I've been here?'

'No,' she said huskily, because if she mentioned him Roland would fly into one of his tempers, and Christabel would much rather pretend she didn't even know Claude de Larzac. She looked up at him with resentful eyes because he had hurt her badly, and because he was trying to trap Roland. 'Why don't you go back to Paris?'

'And leave you to deal with Roland?' he murmured with a smile, watching her face.

'And how exactly does she mean to do that?' asked a harsh voice from the other side of the hall, and they both spun round.

Roland must have come in from the garden door, through the meandering corridors to the kitchen, which was why they had not heard him arrive.

Claude held out a hand, instantly all smiles. 'Roland, my dear! What a pleasure to see you again after so long! How well you look. A good ten years younger! I can see life down here agrees with you!'

'Get out of my house!' Roland snarled, advancing.

Claude's urbane look fell from him like a discarded cloak; he paled and backed, with something rabbitlike about him suddenly.

'Now, my dear,' he bleated, 'be reasonable! I've come a long way to see you, and you might at least listen to what I have to say.'

'Get out before I throw you out!' Roland was a few feet away; his voice made Christabel wince, but Claude didn't run away.

He had no intention of facing Roland, mind you. He had no illusions as to his ability to fight Roland, so he side-stepped behind Christabel, and used her as a shield, his arm clamped around her.

She was so startled that she was too late to stop him, and merely managed a gasped, 'What do you think you're doing?'

Claude took no notice. He was too busy talking urgently to Roland. 'I'm your biggest admirer, Roland, you know that! Why else do you think I'm here? You shouldn't be stuck in this God-forsaken backwater, farming, when you could be where you belong, in Paris, writing. The theatre is crying out for your work. There's nobody living who can hold a candle to you.'

His flattery made no impression on Roland, who was glaring at him with clenched teeth which showed white between his taut lips. He parted them briefly, only to bite out, 'Let go of her, and come out where I can hit you, you cowardly little rat!'

'Yes,' said Christabel, 'let go of me!' She was incensed because neither man was taking any notice of her. Roland looked through her as if she were made of glass, and as for Claude, he didn't care what she thought.

'Paris would be at your feet if you came up with another masterpiece!' Claude had no intention of letting go of her, and when Roland made a grab for his shoulder in an attempt to pull him away from her Claude feverishly whirled out of reach, taking Christabel with him, his body clamped behind her.

She struggled angrily, her face turning white because Roland was looking at her as if he loathed her, and it wasn't fair; she hadn't done anything to him!

'I'll get you!' Roland promised, breathing thickly, his face full of dark red blood and his hands clenching into fists. 'You can't keep out of my way forever, and when I do get my hands on you I'll throttle the life out of you.'

'You know very well I'm not the physical type, never have been! I don't pretend to be one of those macho men who go in for weight-lifting and playing squash. I'm no match for you!' Claude complained bitterly. 'Have the decency to admit...it would be a massacre, and I've no intention of letting you put me through a mincing machine just for kicks, so you can stop breathing hellfire and calling me a coward. I may be a coward, but I'm not a fool. What do you think I would get out of being beaten into a pulp?'

Roland eyed him for a moment, then he smiled twistedly. 'You aren't even worth the effort, are you? Clear off, back to Paris, Larzac!'

He turned his hostile dark eyes to Christabel, stared into her eyes for a long moment, then ran a contemptuous, dismissive gaze over her, from head to foot, a sneer on his mouth. She felt a wave of scarlet flow up to her temples, then the hot colour ebbed away again, leaving her icy cold, trembling and on the point of tears.

'And take her with you!' Roland told Claude without detaching his eyes from her. 'I want her out of my house tonight!'

# CHAPTER NINE

THE tears came then; a blinding rush of tears which Christabel couldn't bear him to see. She fled, a hand over her face, instinctively making for the stairs and her room.

'Oh, don't be a fool!' she heard Claude say to Roland and heard the biting reply.

'I'm not the fool. You are—if you believe I'll have that deceitful little bitch under this roof another instant! I know what your game was! She was another of your decoys, wasn't she? You're so clever, Larzac. I always said you were the best businessman in Paris. You know how to fool an audience, but you've met your match in me. Do you think I ever believed in her? It suited me to let her stay to look after Eve-Marie's brats, but she didn't take me in! I told her the first night she arrived that I knew what she was up to, and I was right, wasn't I?'

Christabel rushed into her bedroom and began pulling her clothes out of cupboards and drawers. She packed without caring whether or not she creased anything. Her hands were shaking and tears ran down her cheeks constantly, but she didn't stop to brush them away until her case was full, and then she stopped, sniffing like a sad child, running her fingers over her wet eyes while she took a last look round the room to make sure she hadn't left anything.

She had been here such a short time, yet so much had happened to her here. She had been wildly happy, she had been intensely miserable—and all because of the stupid, blind, obstinate man downstairs, who could not see ... would not see ... how much she——

She broke off, refusing to finish that sentence, angrily lifting her case off the bed, and turned towards the door. But she couldn't go yet, not just like that. She couldn't leave the children here without saying goodbye to them. They would be worried, upset, even frightened, if she just vanished during the night.

Luckily they were fond of Jeanne now, and they knew their uncle much better, and were quite at home in the *château*—but still, Christabel was their one link with their home, with Paris and their mother.

She put the case down again and quietly opened the connecting door between her room and theirs. Their room was very dark and they were asleep. She hesitated by the two little beds, staring at the children: Dani lay on her side, her hand curled under her cheek, her pink mouth open as she breathed; Nina had her thumb in her mouth and was deeply flushed.

Christabel frowned—did Nina have a temperature? What if she was coming down with some childish ailment like measles? She anxiously leaned over her to feel her forehead, but Nina didn't seem particularly hot to her, the flush wasn't significant.

She couldn't wake them, though. They were too deeply asleep; she couldn't do it to them. She tiptoed out again, quietly closing the door, and picked up her case. She would stay in town tonight at the hotel, and come back tomorrow to say goodbye to the children before going on to England.

She gave her room a final glance, then firmly left it and walked down the stairs. To her surprise she couldn't see Claude as she glanced down the great hall. The front door was shut and Roland was in the hall alone; he had put a match to the fire which Jeanne built every day, but which in summer was only lit occasionally if the weather was bad. Roland had turned out the main lights and only left on a small lamp on a table. The hall was dusky except where the black shadows of the flames leapt up the high walls. Roland stood at the hearth, leaning on the mantelpiece with one hand, his head bent and one foot on the stone steps of the hearth. Firelight carved his profile into an unyielding mask.

'Where is Monsieur de Larzac?' Christabel asked him huskily, after a moment of uncertain silence when Claude did not put in an appearance.

'Gone.' Roland did not look round.

'Gone?' She couldn't understand what he meant; she stood there, clutching her case, staring stupidly. 'Gone where?'

'Who knows?' Roland kicked the fire, sending up a shower of sparks, and she jumped, appalled. 'Who cares?' Roland asked viciously, still without looking at her.

'But . . . but he was going to take me with him . . .' she stammered, frightened of him in this black mood. He radiated violence; he was capable of anything.

'He didn't wait. He took to his cowardly heels and ran, and just as well for him he did—I was thinking of wringing his damned neck.' He still hadn't looked round, his gaze fixed broodingly on the fire. 'If you want to catch up with him, you'd better run fast. He is probably half-way to town by now.'

She bit her lip, not knowing what to do—what did he expect her to do? 'May I ring for a taxi?'

'Where would you want it to take you?'

'Town. The hotel, I suppose.'

'It's gone eleven o'clock. By the time you get to town, it will be midnight. The hotel won't give you a room at that hour.'

Shrilly, she burst out, 'Well, what do you expect me to do? Sleep in a ditch? You told me to leave— where am I to go in the middle of the night?'

'Oh, go back upstairs,' he muttered, his head bent. 'You can leave tomorrow.'

She stood there staring at him for a long moment, struggling with an angry, miserable torrent of words which wouldn't come out. They were dammed up by her knowledge that he wouldn't believe anything she said. He despised her, and she was helpless to defend herself against the things he believed.

'Go on!' he suddenly yelled, lifting his head and turning it to glare, his face harsh and darkly flushed. 'Get out of my sight, for God's sake!'

Christabel almost ran, her heavy case dragging down her arm, making it difficult to climb the stairs. She didn't know if Roland watched her because she couldn't look at him again. She only wanted to be alone to cry where he couldn't see or hear her.

She bolted her door and dropped her case, threw herself on her bed, and let the sobs break out of her shaking body, her face buried in her cover so that she shouldn't disturb the children. She mustn't wake them up; it would frighten them to see her cry. It was almost frightening her. She had never cried like this before. All her tears until now had been childish, easily cried, easily forgotten. She knew that these tears were different. She cried with unbearable intensity and could not stop.

It seemed a long time before the tears were cried out of her. At last she stopped, blew her nose, washed her face, and got undressed before climbing into bed. She put out the light and lay there, knowing she wasn't going to sleep, her thoughts going round and round inside her head like a white mouse in a tiny cage.

Tomorrow she was going away and she would never see him again, and she loved him. How was she going to bear it?

She turned over, sighing heavily. She must go to sleep. But how could she when tomorrow she was going away...?

Round and round in her head the equation went. She no longer wept, but she was intensely unhappy. All the same, somehow, she slowly went to sleep.

She woke up with a start some time during the night and sat up, dazed and half asleep still. What was that?

Something had woken her: a noise, a shout, something strange. She listened and heard it again— a crash, the splintering of breaking glass somewhere downstairs.

Oh, my God! she thought, jumping out of bed. Someone's breaking into a downstairs room! She pulled on a thin silk dressing-gown and ran out of

her room, along the corridor to Roland's room. She
tapped on the door softly. She didn't want to alert
the burglar to the fact that someone had heard him.
Her tap must have been too soft, because Roland
didn't hear it. She tapped again, there was still no
reply, so she carefully opened the door and peered
across the room.

*'Monsieur?'* She could see the darkness of his
hair against the pillow, the shape of his body under
the bedclothes, hear his rhythmic breathing. He
must have been deeply asleep because he didn't
move, and she had to go closer, to put out a ten-
tative hand and touch him.

*'Monsieur?'* she said a little louder, and then he
came awake in a hurry, sitting up, staring at her in
amazement through the darkness.

'What the...?'

Christabel leapt at him and put a hand over his
mouth as the first angry sounds emerged.
'Please...shh...don't make a noise,' she whispered. 'There's someone downstairs!'

He bit her palm. She snatched her hand away,
jumping. 'Tell whoever it is I don't want to see
him!' he snarled.

Bewildered, she stammered, 'No, you don't
understand...I was in bed and I heard noises...'

His face changed. 'What sort of noises?'

'It sounded like a window smashing.'

He swung out of bed, and that was when she
realised at last that he was sleeping naked again.
She hadn't noticed because she'd been so anxious
about the sounds she'd heard. She turned her back
hurriedly and heard a short laugh from him.

'What a contradiction you are!'

She didn't answer or look at him until she heard him putting on clothes. Did he always sleep naked? she wondered, very conscious of his movements.

'It's safe to look at me now,' he told her ironically a moment later, and she turned back to see that he was wearing a long, belted black velvet dressing-gown of magnificent Edwardian design. Her amber eyes widened briefly in a flash of intense attraction, then she looked down, heat flowing into her face, as she met Roland's narrowed gaze.

'Shouldn't we ring the police?' she whispered.

There was an odd silence, and she risked a glance up at him again, through her lashes. Roland was staring down at her, his brows together, his face tautly shadowed. He made her nervous. She wished she knew what he was thinking—hadn't he heard her?

'Shouldn't we ring the police?' she repeated, and he visibly pulled himself together, his mouth indenting with impatience.

'Oh . . . no, not yet. First, I'd better go down and find out if there is an intruder. You wait here.'

'You can't go down there alone, it might be someone violent!' she burst out, paling as she had visions of him being attacked by whoever had broken into the *château*. 'Please, Roland . . . don't . . .' She put a hand on his sleeve and held him back.

He had turned towards his bedroom door, but as she clung to his arm he looked down at her, his face drily amused. 'I can take care of myself! Don't look so scared!' He firmly unpeeled her fingers. 'If I don't call up to tell you everything's OK, ring the police.'

'What's their number?' she asked anxiously, and he gave her a long-suffering look.

'Just get the operator and explain that you need the police, and she'll sort it out.'

He thought she was some sort of half-wit, and how could she blame him when every time he came near her she behaved as if she were bewitched? Well, this was the *Manoir du Sorcier*—and sorcery obviously ran in the Bellème family. Roland had put a spell on her the first time she had seen him, and she didn't think she would ever be free of his magic.

While she was day-dreaming, Roland had gone, she suddenly realised. She ran after him to the door, and was in time to see him disappear down the stairs. Feeling like Alice in Wonderland watching the White Rabbit vanish, Christabel wanted to follow him, but he had told her to ring the police if he didn't give her an all-clear signal, so she had to stay up here, near the phone. She hovered by the door, listening intently and trying to guess what was happening downstairs.

She heard nothing for a moment, then distantly she caught Roland's voice speaking, although she couldn't hear what he said. Christabel's heart beat thickly, she was poised, ready to dash to the phone, but she didn't hear any sounds of fighting, not even raised voices.

Silence had fallen again. She took a step closer to the top of the stairs, biting her lip. What was happening down there? Roland had been gone for ages! She couldn't wait much longer—shouldn't she ring the police now?

She wished she dared put on the lights, but she didn't want to alert the burglars to the fact that there was anyone else up here. First, she must ring the police, then she could go downstairs and try to help Roland. She was about to turn back to the phone when a dark shape moved at the top of the stairs, and Christabel gave a choked scream.

The shape shot towards her, grabbed her, a hand over her mouth to silence her as she had silenced Roland a few moments ago.

She struggled wildly, staring upwards, then stopped fighting as she recognised who held her.

'Don't wake the children, for God's sake! I couldn't cope with them as well!' Roland hissed, and Christabel went limp, her knees giving in relief.

He caught her before she fell, his arm shooting round her waist to support her. She was very cold, her head was swimming, she felt dizzy. She couldn't hold on to consciousness; she felt her sense of herself streaming away like smoke, and fell forwards against him. Roland gave a muffled curse, then slid an arm under her knees and lifted her off the ground easily, her body very small and light in his arms. That was the last thing she knew about.

She must have fainted then, because she knew nothing about how she got there, but when she returned to consciousness she found herself lying on Roland's bed. He was kneeling beside her, gently placing a cold, damp cloth across her temples.

Her lashes fluttered; she stared blankly up at him. 'What happened?'

'You fainted.' He picked up her hands and rubbed them, frowning. 'You're as cold as ice!'

'I meant downstairs! Was it an intruder?'

'In a way,' he told her with wry amusement. 'It was Caesar!'

'Caesar?' She closed her eyes, groaning. 'Oh, no! Was that all?'

'I'm afraid so! I forgot to put him out in his kennel. He was in the kitchen, and he must have seen a mouse, or thought he did, because he climbed up on the table and knocked a glass on to the floor. Luckily, he hadn't cut himself, so I told him what I thought of him, cuffed him and put him out, then swept up the glass before I came back up here, only to have you scream and faint on me!'

Confused, she looked away, pulling her hands out of his grasp. 'I thought you were the burglar.'

'I did manage to work that out!' He removed the damp cloth from her forehead. 'How do you feel? You went as white as a sheet, but you've got more colour now.'

She couldn't look at him—his nearness had so powerful an effect on her senses that she was terrified he would see it in her eyes. 'I'm fine now. I'm sorry I raised the alarm for nothing.'

'Don't be silly!' he said roughly, frowning. 'If I'd heard a glass break downstairs, I would have reacted just the way you did. It could just as easily have been a burglar.'

'Well...thanks,' she said, nervously sitting up, very aware of how little she was wearing, even more conscious of the fact that under his dressing-gown Roland was naked. She had to get out of the room fast. She held her thin rose-pink silk wrap together and tried to slide off the bed, but Roland caught hold of her shoulders, pressing her backwards again.

'No, lie still! You ought to take a moment or two to get over that faint. Would you like a glass of water?'

'Yes, please,' she said, shivering at the touch of his hands, hoping he would have to go downstairs to get it and that would give her a chance to escape.

But he simply picked up a glass from his bedside-table, filled it from a jug of iced water standing beside it, then slipped a hand under her head to lift it from the pillow, and held the glass to her lips.

Christabel tried to stop trembling, but she couldn't. Her teeth knocked against the glass and she felt Roland watching her intently. She drank a little; the water was very cold and her throat seemed very hot.

Roland put the glass down on the table again, but he didn't remove his hand from under her head. His fingers stayed, softly caressing the warm nape of her neck, under her hair, sending shudders of deep awareness through her.

'I wanted to kill you earlier,' he said thickly, watching her with brooding dark eyes. 'When you first came, I thought you were here to try and seduce me, but it seemed so unbelievable—I couldn't see Larzac sending someone like you, a quiet little English girl, neat and brown, like a sparrow, with no sex appeal and no idea how to make a man look twice at her!'

'Thanks,' she muttered bitterly.

He touched her cheek with his free hand, the sound of a smile in his voice. 'Did that sting? What do you want me to say? That you're a raving beauty? But you're not, Bel, and if you were I wouldn't want you anywhere near me. I've learnt that surfaces are deceptive. I've learnt to look underneath.'

She was listening so intently that she didn't realise where his hand was going as it moved away from her face. One minute it was stroking her cheek, the next it was sliding inside her robe, and she gasped in shock as she felt his fingertips brush the hollow between her small breasts.

'Oh . . .' she mouthed, stiffening.

Roland's eyes had a heated, passionate darkness in them. 'My wife was all surface. Pretty as a picture, isn't that what the English say? Oh, she was lovely to look at—but she was a bitch, and she made me the laughing-stock of Paris. I was such a blind fool that I didn't even guess she was sleeping with half my friends. I was the only one who didn't know what was going on!'

Christabel caught hold of his hand and pushed it away. She tried to sit up again, and Roland said absently, 'Stay where you are! You might faint again.'

She didn't argue because she was deeply interested in what he was telling her. Something had occurred to her. 'Maybe she wanted to get your attention? That's why children are often naughty, just to make you take notice of them.'

He grimaced. 'A psychiatrist suggested the same thing when I asked him why she should have been that way. He said it was what made her an actress; she was an exhibitionist, she hungered for attention.'

Huskily, Christabel said, 'So she did really love you, underneath——'

'No, she loved herself,' Roland said flatly. 'She was a sick woman, I suppose. She had to make every man she met want her...even my own brother!'

Christabel ached with pity for him, and in a strange way she felt real pity for his dead wife, too. She couldn't imagine how any woman could live with herself if she had acted that way, but Roland was right. His wife must have been a sick woman.

'I'm so sorry, I wish there was something I could do...' she whispered, and Roland gave her a long, strange look, then smiled.

'There is,' he said, his hands back inside her robe the next instant, and softly probing under the clinging silk of her nightdress to cup her breasts.

She gave a cry of helpless arousal, her eyes closing, pleaded wordlessly, shaking her head, and he bent over her, his mouth teasing, lightly brushing her lips, her chin, her throat.

She loved him so badly, but she knew he didn't love her. He had been honest about that. She was plain and had no sex appeal, but he wanted a woman, and she was a woman and she was there, available.

That was what hurt most—that he knew how she felt about him, that he knew how much she wanted him to make love to her, and was prepared to take advantage of that.

'How can you?' she muttered, the sound of tears in her voice, tears burning behind her lids. 'You're acting the way she did...using me...the way she used men——'

He went rigid, his lean body lifting away so that he could stare down at her white face.

'*No!* My God, Bel, how can you think I'd do that to you?' He took her shoulders and shook her violently, but this was one time when he wasn't going to frighten her into backing off.

'Do you think I don't know you're still in love with her?' she accused unsteadily, and Roland stared into her amber eyes, his own hard and narrowed.

'You're crazy!'

'No, it isn't me who's crazy,' she said, her mouth trembling, her eyes glazed with unshed tears. 'I'm very sane, and I'm very rational. That's the way I've been brought up. I was taught to be independent from an early age, and to use my brains. I may be young—I can't help being young, and time will deal with that problem, anyway—but if there is one thing I'm certain about it's that you are still carrying a torch for your wife. I understand all of it . . . why you won't go back to Paris, why you have that portrait of her up in your tower, why you didn't want anyone to know you still have pictures of her around, why you look at me with contempt when you're sober, and when you're drunk make passes at me——' She broke off, swallowing, and Roland tried to put his arms around her, his face taut.

'Bel! Listen——'

'No, you listen to me! You still love her, but you're alive and you're a man, and you need a woman now and then——'

He made a sound between rough laughter and a groan. 'My God, Bel! The things you say! You just don't understand——'

'I do!' she insisted. 'I understand. I'm not as dumb as you seem to think I am! And I'm not prudish ... but ...' she swallowed again, her mouth very dry, her tongue-tip moistening her lips before she could get the words out '... but I ... couldn't ... I'd hate myself forever if I did ... So I'm sorry, but the answer is no!'

'OK, I've listened to you, Bel. Now, will you let me finally say a word in my own defence?'

She bowed her head, nodding it.

'First, then, I stopped loving my wife soon after her death. It was shock enough to find out that she had been having an affair with my brother, but then I found a diary she had been keeping for years. I read it in a state of utter shock. I kept telling myself she had invented most of it, I couldn't believe what I was reading, but then I slowly realised it was true. All of it. For years I had been living with a total stranger, and my marriage had been a lie.'

'You hadn't had any suspicions until then?' she whispered incredulously, and Roland laughed shortly.

'That was something I got asked over and over again. By the police, by the coroner at the inquest, by her family, by my friends ... I can only give you the answer I gave them. No, I had no suspicions—either about my brother, or any of the others. From time to time, it's true, I did wonder if she still loved me. I wondered if I still loved her. But I didn't look too closely because, I suppose, I was afraid of what I'd find, and that is a failure I do blame myself for. Maybe my indifference was what pushed her further and further over the edge. I should never have married her. I thought I loved her at the time, I thought she loved me—but the truth is our marriage didn't work out. We weren't happy, although

I was never prepared to admit it. I just kept hoping it would change one day. I thought if she had a baby——'

'That never works,' Christabel said sadly. 'Having a baby just to stick a marriage back together again never works.'

'No, you're right,' he agreed. 'She didn't want one, anyway. She didn't like children.'

'Oh,' she said, biting her bottom lip, then she gave him a quick glance, frowning. 'But if you weren't still in love with her, why did you leave Paris?'

'Because I was bored with living there!' he said drily and her amber eyes opened wide.

'Bored? With Paris?'

He laughed at the incredulity. 'Yes, *chérie*. With Paris! I was homesick, I wanted to come back here, where I belonged, and I wanted to work on my own land, the land my family had been working for generations. I am a Breton. I'm not a Parisian, and maybe part of my soul is puritan, but I found corruption in Paris, and I wanted no more of it. Here the wind blows fiercely and it is often bitterly cold. We have thick mists in spring and autumn, even in summer! But the air is clean and I can smell the sea and look at the great, open sky. This is where I belong.'

'But the theatre?'

'I ran out of ideas, *chérie*. That was all. One day my head was empty and I had nothing more to say on a stage.'

Doubtfully, she said, 'Nothing to do with your wife?'